Free the Giraffes

by

Nick Delmedico
and
R. R. Harrison

A division of d+2

Manufactured in the United States of America

Free the Giraffes
Fiction, Fantasy

ISBN 978-1-58884-017-2

"If we have not found the heaven within, we have not found the heaven without."

- James Hilton

0

In the future there will be intentional communities, isolated pockets of people gathered together to support each other in spiritual and altruistic values. They will be founded on higher principles: sustainability, consciousness, and community. These places exist today, struggling in their infancy. What will these communities look like in a hundred or more years? Our hopes and our imagination tell us that the seeds we plant today will grow into something that could nourish our bodies and our souls, aligning mankind's destiny with the divine plan, whatever that might be.

Meanwhile, the world struggles with a system based on vastly different values. I won't try to define them, the world is what it is, but change cannot occur if we don't experiment with new ways of living. That is the primary mission of many of these communities, to experiment and pave the way for change, to discover new ways of living in harmony with the Earth and with each other.

This is the story of one such community, spiritually awakened and ready for the challenges that may come in the future.

1

"Come on, Anji. We're both awake. Time to run."

Randall reached around the neck of the giraffe, hugging it gently. He squeezed slightly, a signal for the animal to pick up speed.

"Come on, Anji. let's get a move on. Hyah!"

Anji snorted, cantered, then broke into a full run. Randall looked around from the perch on her back, the sea to his right, the city to his left, the giraffe beneath him. This is what life was about for him, enjoying a morning ride along the beach on his giraffe. He wore the robes of a holy man, for that is what he was, a sacred rider at one with his world and his mount. He rode past the marina, past the kayak rentals, zipping past the power plant that gently milked the waves and the sun for energy. He slowed as they passed the dense resort area, early morning tourists rising out of their chairs to peek out from under their umbrellas and stare at the odd sight of a mounted rider on a giraffe.

A child pointed and laughed. "Look, Mama," he said. "Can I ride a giraffe, too?"

"It doesn't look safe," she said, Randall towering nearly ten feet above them. "Maybe when you're older."

The city loomed to his left. Randall could think of no other place on Earth that he wanted to live. He had a vision when he was young about starting a spiritual community, a place based on sustainability, a city far from the values of the common world. And here it was, the Eighth Day Village of the Sun, a dream come true.

This was not an ordinary city. There were buildings unlike any seen before. Some were organic and grown or made from plants, some were open, temporary structures with people living in them, some were low and flat, blending into the landscape with natural cover. There were pyramids and ziggurats, columned temples, spired churches and grand meeting halls. The mountains behind the city were towering, a waterfall dropping thousands of feet into a lake littered with exotic watercraft. Near the waterfall, animals lounged in the morning sun. Further up the cliff a mountain lion sat on a ledge. Birds were everywhere, their chirping creating a symphony of sound that soothed the spirit.

Randall was One with all this beauty. It could not be otherwise.

There was a shout from behind him. "Baba Randall! They are here! Baba Randall Can you hear me? Stop, please!"

Randall recognized the voice, his personal assistant Ravi calling to him about something important. Randall was the founder of the village as well as the head of it, always in demand for one thing or another. He ignored Ravi, pretending he didn't hear. Whatever it was, it would keep for a while. "Hyah, Anji!"

Ahead at a thatch-roofed beach bar Manny heard the shouts, the sound of approaching giraffe hooves. He looked up and smiled, cut his conversation short with a tourist and turned to prepare a fresh mango smoothie. The giraffe slowed and stopped beside the bar, her tall head dipping in the early sun, braying as Randall pet her gently. "Good girl, Anji. Good girl."

Manny stepped out from behind the bar grabbing an odd device: a serving tray attached to a long pole. He placed the smoothie carefully on the tray and raised it up for the mounted rider to take.

Randall picked up the tall glass and drank deep, then held it to his forehead where it cooled his sweating brow. He pulled it away and took another drink. "Ahh. Delicious. Thank you Manny," he said.

Manny smiled and pointed at the stretch of shoreline behind him. "You know Ravi has been chasing you down the beach again."

"Yes. One day he will figure out that a human can't run faster than a giraffe." Randall shook his head and took another drink. "How about you, Manny? How are you coming with your research?"

"Fine, fine," said the bartender. "You were right to point me towards basic particle physics. I've developed a few instruments to measure the capture potential of certain crystals. A network of these crystals deployed across Gaia can act as positive energy vortexes, maybe even heal areas of the Earth we thought beyond help. I'm having great success growing crystals for this project."

Randall shook his head. "Honestly, Manny. I don't know why you don't quit bartending and join us in the Think Tank up on the hill."

Manny laughed. "Now why would I do that? Who would make your mango smoothie in the morning? Besides, here with the tourists I have a better chance of meeting my future wife." He winked, a secret signal that made Randall smile.

"So you do, so you do," he said. He took one last drink, put the glass back on the tray. Manny took the glass, set it in the sink behind the bar where he returned to the tourist, eager to listen to what she had to say.

Ravi arrived, out of breath. "Baba Randall. We need you," he said. "They're coming. You said they would come. You said they would come!"

Randall pretended he didn't hear. "Ah! Good morning Ravi." He knew what was happening, but he didn't let it interfere with his morning ride.

Ravi was excited. "They're almost here, Baba Randall."

"Who, Ravi? Who's almost here?"

"The committee. The representatives of the world. They have come here needing our help. Beyond our walls there is chaos, if we believe the news feeds."

Randall looked off into space. "Then it's beginning. The collapse of the world."

Ravi smiled. "Yes. Just as you predicted, Baba Randall. You must be happy to be vindicated."

Randall frowned. "No, I would have much preferred a soft landing to the chaos. Chaos is nothing to smile about, Ravi. The world is suffering right now. Time to fulfill our destiny."

Ravi hid his smile, looking serious now. "Yes, Baba Randall. But think about it. Who could they turn to? Think about your own struggle, how you planned for this day. How you built the Eighth Day Village of the Sun from nothing. Without their help."

Randall continued to look off into the distance as he spoke. "I respect the government and they respect me. I always knew they would need us when their backs were against the wall."

Ravi continued. "You built this city. Then you built New Maya City of Worlds, our sister city. And now those who sought to stop you come to ask you for help."

"And we must give it to them, Ravi. Just not in the manner they expect."

"Yes, but think about it! Remember how it all started?"

"I remember, Ravi," he said. He stared out across the water. "Oh yes, I remember."

2

He was quite young at the time, his rakish good looks accented by his trimmed beard and pointed mustache. Women liked to comment on his tight denim jeans, tilted stetson hat, and custom made aqua blue cowboy boots that he always wore. His tanned skin and toothy smile set them at ease. He had the gift of conversation and the ability to talk about any subject. Even back then he had a *presence*. But unlike most young men, interests of the flesh were furthest from Randall's mind. He preferred spending his mornings in peaceful meditation, a passive exercise that had occupied his mind for many years.

On this particular day he had a breakthrough. It started as a struggle. Deep in his heart there was turmoil, the pain of the world, Tears of the Masters bled from his chest. By those that know, the state is often called Christ Consciousness, where one feels the suffering of humanity as if their own. The Sacred Heart of Christ burned in his chest. The fire traveled up his spine and a bright light exploded on the top of his head. From the top of his scalp a golden cord emerged, a shimmering rope that stretched heavenward.

He blinked his eyes, and suddenly he was outside of himself looking down at his meditative form. The golden cord beckoned him and he stared up trying to see where it led. It was hard to see, the light was bright and blinding as if he were looking up into the sun. He decided to climb the cord. Like Jack and the beanstalk, he ascended into the mystic, the clouds parting ever so gently to illuminate him on his journey. He climbed for what seemed like hours, the struggle making him weary until he reached up one time and found not rope, but solid ground to grab. He pulled himself up, twisting and rolling to a seated position.

"About time you got here," said a gentle voice beside him.

He looked over, staring into the sun itself, the source of all the blinding light. "Who are you?" he asked.

The voice answered him. "You don't recognize your own soul? Your own beginning and end?"

Randall squinted, seeing features he recognized come into focus. It was like looking into a mirror, a golden one that somehow radiated light. There was no denying. "I thought as much," he said. "Is God here too?"

"Of course, present in our hearts, and in everything around us," said the voice. "I'm glad that you are here. Why did you come?"

"Where else is there to go?" answered Randall. "There is no other journey worth taking."

His soul stared back and laughed at him.

"What are you laughing at?" asked Randall "I'm not the only one looking in a mirror. I get this sense of humor from you, don't I?"

"Yes, you do," said the voice. "And now that you're here, I have something to give you."

The bright being stretched out his hand where it held a transparent box. Randall was drawn into it. He saw layers of complexity within it, architectural plans, work schedules, personnel lists, images of buildings, financial budgets and even glimpses of people. The box trembled like Pandora's, wanting to be free and have a life of its own. Randall took it without hesitation.

"I've seen this before," he said.

"Yes, you have," said the golden voice.

"Deja vu." He stared into the cube, layers of complexity opening to him like a lotus flower. He looked up at his soul into deep, bright eyes of compassion fixing their gaze on him. "I seem to remember talking to you about this before. Dream time learning?" he asked.

There was no answer, and time spent with the soul, though infinite, is still finite. His soul drew attention to the cube again. "You'll know what to do with it. Off you go, now. I'm busy trying to awaken a primitive version of us in the distant past. If I succeed you will find that we have twice the psychic ability in your time."

"How do you do that?" asked Randall.

"It's not important," he said. "You'll find out one day. See you again, my little fragment."

With that, Randall slipped away, sliding down the golden chord until he thumped back into his own head. His eyes opened in astonishment, the cube reflected in his retina, burned into his mind.

"I better get busy," he said.

It took years, talking, writing books, grants, podcasts, blogs, any way to get the word out, but Randall was obsessed with creating an intentional community, a place where spiritual minded people could live, work, and worship with the faith of their choice in the manner of their choosing. There had to be other people who felt the same way. He started with a tour of conference rooms at major hotels across the world where he presented his ideas. He hoped to meet people who would share his vision and help him build his village.

He wasn't sure it would work. He stood at the podium, a large screen behind him flashing images, crude recreations of pictures from the cube. They didn't glow with light and life like the ones given to him by his soul, but they made the point. Still, few people had come forward to help. He felt like a modern day curiosity, a soon to be forgotten zoo animal that people came to see and discuss later at their leisure.

The audience was sparse, and he had already decided that the little bit of money he had was better spent directly on his ideas rather than traveling around and talking about them. He had the thought over morning tea to cancel the rest of his tour and return home and focus on the work that needed to be done. He wrapped up his speech, the last of his slides showing his vision for the Eighth Day Village of the Sun.

"Thank you all for attending," he said. "Please be aware that the current world system is unsustainable. The bubble must burst one day. The only safe place will be intentional communities. Please consider this information and follow my blog on the website. Most of all, I encourage you to take action."

The applause was weak. He gathered up his material and put it in the open briefcase beside him. A small group of people crowded around him, the usual flock of onlookers asking pointed questions, demands for autographs for his books, and the jaded few who tried to blast holes in his theories. He prepared for the onslaught, catering to their petty desires, their need for attention and the countless questions, always the same, always leading to the same results. A few donations but never enough to cover his expenses.

He autographed the book, answered a quick question, then looked into the eyes of bright young man standing off to the side. The young man patiently waited his turn, then stepped forward and greeted him as if he were an on old, dear friend.

"Do I know you?" he asked.

"I've been waiting to talk to you, Randall," said the bright young man. "I've been following your work for some time."

"Have we met somewhere before?" asked Randall, the signs of recognition growing between them as he searched his past. And suddenly there was a flash of insight, an image of the young man in the cube stack during the conversation with his soul. A name came to mind as he focused on the memory that appeared in the form of a personnel list. "Doctor Darius?" he asked.

The young man smiled. "Yes," he said. "My friends call me Darius, but I'm not a doctor. Not yet, anyway."

Randall took his hand, felt the strength and energy from it. "What did you want to talk about?" he asked.

Darius held out a sheaf of papers. "This," he said.

Randall skimmed through the papers, a portfolio of pictures that resembled the images he had just projected on the viewscreen during his lecture. He turned and looked at the large screen behind him comparing the image to the crude representation of his village. "So?" he asked. "You downloaded a few pictures from my website, photo-shopped the images. They're pretty. Is this what you wanted to talk about?"

Darius smiled. "Look closely," he said. "Some of these views are not quite the same as yours. And your power plant did not have a detailed engineering sketch of a torus shaped power generator."

He pulled a picture out from the portfolio and pointed to it. Randall took the picture and studied it closely. "This appears to be an improved hybrid torus energy plant."

"Yes, said Darius. "A torus. A doughnut shaped thing that uses gravo-magnetic power to make electricity."

16

"Where did you get this?" asked Randall.

"It came to me in a vision," said Darius.

"Did it look anything like this?" Randall dug into the bottom of his briefcase and produced a sheaf of papers of his own. The cover bore the title "Free the Giraffes." Darius took the paperwork, a polished, bound copy of Randall's plan. He thumbed through it. It was bursting with pictures, lists, columns of figures and schedules. Darius studied the detailed designs comparing them to the ones he had in a bound report of his own. He finally stopped on a page with an ominous figure in bold print that said: "FINAL PROJECTED SIX YEAR COST $630 million dollars US."

"How are we going to pay for all this Randall?" asked Darius.

It was the way he said it, using the word *we*, as if he were already a member of Randall's team. "*We* don't have to pay for it all at once," he said. "I have some land and a few holdings. I planned on starting small, maybe in Mexico, Costa Rica, or some other friendly, industrialized nation."

"That could work," said Darius. "We could develop the site in phases. Start with five buildings. Besides housing, what do you think we should build first?"

The answer came quick as Randall replied, "An air conditioned conference center."

3

Baba Randall stood just inside the doorway staring at the dimly lit air conditioned conference room. His presence activated the motion detectors and the lights in the room slowly illuminated the intricate details. The room was stunning, immaculately staged and decorated, harmonious in form and substance. A row of shaded windows looked out towards the lagoon. Along the back wall was an array of monitors and display screens. Large and elaborate crystals rested in carved cubbie holes. Plants and vegetation filled the remaining empty spaces. The chairs were plush and comfortable, arranged around a large, polished oval table roughly in the center of the room. Computer screens were embedded in the table. The illumination from overhead added a soft glow to the room.

He felt a hand on his shoulder. Randall turned to look into the eyes of Doctor Darius.

"I laughed when you said the first thing we had to build was a conference center."

"We've improved it over the years," said Baba Randall. "The tourists and business retreats paid for most of it. Besides selling our excess power, tourism has been the greatest contribution to our economy."

Darius patted him gently on the shoulder. "The team is on their way, Baba."

Randall smiled wide with anticipation. Darius touched a wall panel. The room came to life, lighting up fully as two people entered and took their place at the large round table. Wall mounted monitors lit up to show data and maps, camera feeds from the village and the airport, even the daily menu at the Bhakti Kitchen.

Randall looked over at one of the monitors as it showed a view of the city from offshore. The Crystal Mountain towered high in the background, the beach stretching like a ribbon of white along the shore. Below the beach an azure sea lay tranquil, waves gently lapping against the sand. The monitor next to it cycled through images of their sister city, "New Maya, City of Worlds", the words plainly written at the bottom of the screen. This city was set in a jungle environment, deep green and brown colors complimenting the gray stone used in the construction of the dwellings. Wood and crystal buildings rose above the trees and vines that circled the city. Walkways threaded through the treetops, crowded with people going about their daily business. Dirigibles floated in the sky, islands in the air that were as much a part of the city as the stone and crystal skyscrapers.

Randall turned as Nan Chi Han entered, confident and seductive, exuding femininity. She lit the room brighter than the solar lights that reflected off the finely polished table. Dr. Stine was at her side, a rugged, dark haired man with intense brown eyes. Nan attempted to strike up a pleasant conversation with Randall and Darius as they loitered by the door.

"How we doing, boys?" she said playfully. "You're looking grim today."

"In case you haven't heard, Nan, the world is in economic turmoil," said Darius. "Governments are collapsing faster than the economy. People are dying. It's the corporations that are surviving, feeding off their hoarded resources. But their coffers are draining quicker than they anticipated, and the value of paper money is

19

shrinking."

"Nonetheless, this was foreseen," said Stine. "And now, an emissary of these corporations is coming to visit us, along with a few representatives of their lackey governments."

"Don't forget the Church," said Darius.

"You mean Cardinal Jameson?" laughed Stine. "He's more of an accountant than a spiritual leader."

Randall interrupted. "Remember, these are our misguided brothers and sisters and not our enemies. We must return them to the light. Now is the time."

"Of, course, Baba Randall," said Nan.

As they talked, people continued to enter the room and sit around the table. Ravi finally approached Randall. "Sorry to interrupt, but we are ready."

Ravi took his place behind a podium and activated teleswitches as everyone gathered around the table. A large monitor flickered and then settled on a view of the group. "Teleconferencing system activated," he said. "We're on the air." One of the larger monitors flickered. There was a group of people seated around a similar table, words in block letters at the bottom reading "New Maya Council of Elders."

Ravi nodded. "The meeting is called to order. Let's start with a roll call."

"I think we know everyone here," said Randall. "I've known you all for a long time, trusted members of the Think Tank."

Ravi frowned, used to Randall's comments and interruptions. The holy man realized what he had done. Embarrassed, he excused himself and bowed graciously towards Ravi. "But of course, let us follow formalities. If I may, Ravi."

Randall began to introduce each of them, trusted friends and leaders who helped him shape and guide the community. "First, Mel Ewing, Engineer and designer of our energy systems, waste processing plants, and emergency shelters and habitat." Mel nodded, his stylishly unstyled hair looking like a garden of dark brown spikes on his head.

"Nan Chi Han, Agricultural specialist, feeding the masses through innovation." Randall nodded affectionately towards her as the camera passed over her and on to the next member of the Think Tank. "Barclay McKenner, Theoretical Physicist, Economist, Mathematician, representing the best in scientific modeling." Barclay smiled, his skin tanned and his hair blond from years of exposure to the tropical sun. His white teeth glistened, a sparkle that was matched by his deep, loving eyes.

Next to him was a woman with long dark hair, her golden robes surrounding her like the wrapper on a party favor. "Juliana, you are beautiful today, a Moon Child who glows like the sun," said Randall. He cast her a warm smile, then shared it with the gathering. "Juliana is our High Priestess, and our direct contact with Gaia."

Juliana accepted Randall's compliment modestly and with a demure smile, casting a sly glance at the man sitting beside her.

Randall continued. "Next to her we have Gerald Stine, Geneticist, Deep Time Ecologist, Enlightened Master. Then there is Cameron Singh, reincarnated Atlantean, technology reboot specialist, and our liaison with the Galactics. And finally Darius, our chief architect, visionary, financier, and treasurer." Having finished, Randall turned towards the podium. "And, of course, Ravi, my Aide, confidante and lover. This is our guiding body, but we welcome all of you who may be watching on our live feed. Transparency of leadership is the key to community, just as

21

important as participation in your Government. We welcome your comments and encourage you to provide feedback. Your texts will be read, analyzed, and appended to the minutes of this meeting. Ravi, continue if you please."

"Thank you, Baba Randall, for those introductions. We are assembled today as the core team here at Eighth Day Village of the Sun. We, and the world, are in a state of emergency. We are needed now more than ever." He drew attention to the monitors as he pushed buttons on the podium in front of him. Images of the Village faded, replaced with news feeds showing world chaos: panicked crowds, jammed highways, dead livestock, depressed stock market figures, reports of military coups, natural disasters, and conflict after conflict, the world at war.

Ravi continued. "These news reports only confirm what we have learned through our meditations. The world is in turmoil. We knew when we founded this community that this day would come, and we have planned for it. Nevertheless, humanity needs us now. I must ask you to keep your minds and hearts open." He took a drink of water and a deep breath before continuing. In the silence the news feeds on the monitors drove the point home. Tragedy after tragedy passed before their eyes on the screens.

Ravi cleared his throat, drawing their attention away from the monitors. Juliana crossed her hands in front of her, covering the screen embedded in the tabletop. The frightening images peeked out from between her arms, a vision that, once seen, refused to go away. Ravi clicked a switch, returning the wall to the previous scans of the Village and her sister city. Silence ruled the table. Their faces were empty, some gray, some white, all with downcast, sodden eyes. Stine clutched at his heart with his right hand, a pain that was more than physical. Barclay wiped a tear away with his sleeve, trying to appear calm and in control. Baba Randall pursed his lips, blew a hollow breath and a long sigh. For once he had nothing to say.

Ravi took control of the meeting again. "A contingency of delegates is on their way to visit. They represent world governments, industry, and religion. If you will, please focus again on the monitors." As he spoke, a picture of each individual appeared on the large wall monitors and on the screens embedded in the table in front of each of the attendees. The image of a gaunt man was first, gray hair and gray, shallow eyes, he looked exhausted by life, sucked of energy to the core. "This is Chase Rockefeller," said Ravi. "He represents the banking system. Money has become worthless since it's value has plummeted. Wall Street no longer needs his services, and there is no government rich enough to bail out the banks this time. He is most concerned about continuity and is likely to resist change."

A new picture appeared, a youngish man, his hair dark and polished, every bit in place. "Franklin Van Dorn, a lackey if ever there was one. His thinking is barely fourth dimensional and he has not embraced Christ Consciousness. He is concerned with the future of oil and the industries that it supports."

Darius spoke up. "You remember he was the one who rejected our proposal to provide free, clean energy. All we asked was to stop the drilling and extraction of Gaia's resources."

Ravi moved on to the next photo, a broad man with an iron jawbone, his eyes steel blue, sharp and keen. He wore a uniform. "General Carson Whiteweather, recently appointed head of the U.S. Military. He is loyal to the President, saved him from a military coup twice. He controls the world's largest military machine including a nuclear arsenal that could obliterate two thirds of the world at the push of a button. He is dangerous, preferring to conquer others rather than rule and restrain himself."

"We are not the only ones aware of the problem. The nuclear situation is being monitored by the Galactics as well," said Cameron Singh. "I have been assured that should the need arise, the arsenal will be neutralized and Gaia will be protected along with the innocent."

Ravi nodded, as did several around the table. Juliana voiced the unspoken words on everyone's mind. "Well, that's a relief."

"Next, Cardinal Jameson, personally appointed by the Pope to make sure the Church is represented. The Vatican denounced our practices several times, deeming us a Pagan Community founded by a bunch of over-educated Bohemians. This, despite the fact that we have churches and temples in our cities dedicated to most every faith supported by humanity, including their own. Observe this: They are hesitant to open their bank accounts and lend help to the world, despite being a religious organization. And so, they turn to us, asking us to pour everything we have into saving the world. Intelligence and analysis tell us the Church views this as an opportunity to deplete our resources and with that our strength."

"They realize we are the only ship left to set sail on," said Stine.

"Despite their apparent opposition to us, I believe the Church, or any religious organization, can be our ally in this cause," said Baba Randall. "The people need places to pray together. They need spiritual leaders and the guidance of God."

"Let's just flip the Church into Christ Consciousness for the first time ever," said Juliana.

There was mild laughter around the table before Ravi continued.

"Next, Premier Kenji Alamoto representing the African Block. When the Muslim world refused to help him he asked the Americans for help. Sadly, most of the Americas have problems of their own. The West had also asked the Sheikhs for help and been refused. After many years of meddling, the Muslim World has grown tired of the West and their predominantly Christian influence. An old enmity has reemerged, and the infidels have been left to deal with their own problems. We don't know much about this man Kenji. He recently rose to power by overthrowing several dictators and consolidating his empire. We are currently researching him."

The image changed, replaced by a middle aged woman, light brown hair and matching eyes, her smile escaping through thin upturned lips. "Julie Ann Carver, the only woman in the group. She is a writer by profession, author of many books on a wide variety of subjects including human rights. She is open minded and may be an ally to our cause, if not a possible member of this community. Be mindful dealing with her, she is a master of words. She holds the public's eye and can twist a story in any direction."

An aged and portly man filled the screen, tiny eyes lost between rolls of cheek fat. His look was stern, his mouth tightly clenched by a locked jaw. "T. Harmon Rothschild," said Ravi. "I know what you're thinking. Yes the T stands for "The", T. Harmon Rothschild himself is coming here."

Stine said it first, his voice coming out in a murmur. "The most powerful man in the world."

"And the richest," added Darius. "What's he in for?"

"We are unsure," said Ravi. "Except that he is picking up the tab for this expedition. Transportation costs, food, accommodations. They will all be staying at the Reiki Spa and Resort, our most expensive property."

"That figures," said Barclay. "Nothing but the best for the world's elite."

"I would have figured him to flee to New Zealand with the rest of the super rich," said Stine.

"Me too," said Mel. "They poured millions into buying property there and building hidden bunkers on it. Nice place to wait out any apocalypse."

"I'm sure a lot of them are already there," said Darius. "Fleeing the peasant uprising."

Ravi cleared his throat. "Finally, Sun Ki Han."

There was an audible gasp from Nan.

Ravi continued without interruption. "Han was once director of the Feed Asia program, personally responsible for raising the health and nutritional level of thousands of people. He failed to see the weaknesses of Genetically Modified Organisms. The result has been the elimination of thousands of strains of food crops through their inability to reproduce. All for the fear of losing control of an industry that serves the basic human need of eliminating hunger."

Juliana stared into space. "Sun Ki Han. Why does that name sound so familiar?"

"Sun was once married to our own Nan Chi Han who still bears his surname," said Stine.

"Yes," said Randall. "Do you have any problem with seeing him again, Nan?"

"No, Baba Randall. We dissolved our relationship years ago. We met in graduate school and shared similar interests. We conducted research and published together. We were wed just after graduation, before we started working for the IAC, the International Agriculture Consortium. We talked about raising a family. Sun was not interested in a family and as his career took off, so did he. Fame had a different effect on him than it did me, and after a few dull years we parted amicably."

"I see," said Randall.

"Any other questions about the visiting dignitaries?" asked Ravi.

"The presence of Harmon Rothschild on this expedition somehow disturbs me," said Barclay.

"Explain, Dr. McKenner," said Randall.

"Well, didn't he offer to buy us out at one time?" he asked.

"And we told him no," said Darius. "Gods, man, do you think we'd sell our soul to the devil?"

"Remember what I said, Darius. All of you," said Randall. "These are our lost brothers and sisters, not yet awakened to their potential. We must roll them over. This is our best chance because they all, each and every one of them, will become benevolent when I'm done with them. Watch!"

"Our angelic teams warn me that one of them will attempt to steal our technologies," said Juliana.

"They would use our tools to profit and control the population again," said Mel.

"This will simply reset the broken system that's led to the present problem, with the same eventual outcome," said Stine.

"It has to be Rothschild," said Darius. "Who else would do that? That's why he's paying the bill. They're just here to spy on us."

"Now, now. Let's not go jumping to conclusions," said Randall.

"Yes, but consider this," said Barclay, his analytical powers driving his statements. "What happens when the richest man in the world, used to getting everything he wants, suddenly doesn't get what he wants?"

There was silence as they considered everything they had heard. "Something to ponder, but do it quickly. This group is headed towards our borders, slated to arrive in less than forty minutes. If you will look at your monitors one more time you will see the tour route from the airport leading to the resort at the end. We planned for a dinner later tonight at our own Bhakti Kitchen." A map of the community appeared on the main monitor, the route conspicuously marked.

"We're taking them past the factories?" asked Nan.

"And the gardens, the refugee camps, the machine shops. We have nothing to hide," said Ravi. He nodded to Baba Randall, indicating the meeting was done.

Randall took the cue. "Thank you, Ravi," he said. "One more item before we adjourn to the customs house. Let me stress a few rules of engagement when we greet these people. As always, per our agreement with the Galactics, all anti gravitation devices and practices must be hidden. This includes vehicles as well as the anti gravity scaffolds we use during certain phases of construction. Transportation will use solar powered and electric cars, the magnetic induction public monorail, and, for tomorrow's tour, the battery powered, low altitude transport drones. Answer all questions directly, remembering our security protocols. Trust our system of values. It is much different from the world's, and it has been our stability and our blessing. Keep your psychic senses keen, look past the darkness in their hearts and focus on the light. I think we all know that we will do our best to help them, but maybe not in the way they expect."

"I have a report," said Ravi. "They are ahead of schedule. The plane has landed."

"Time to adjourn," said Randall, adding his customary blessing as the last words. "Ajo, Om Shanti."

4

The airport was on the other side of a mountain range, separated from the city by a sheer wall of stone thousands of feet high. There were few buildings in this valley, mostly fields of crops. Daylight shone brightly above, illuminating the people that worked in the fields. In the distance a tractor gently tilled up new soil, a small crowd following it planting by hand. It was the way of the community. Machinery could till the Earth but it was the human element that made the food grow. A planting ritual was necessary, hands blessed as they carefully placed fresh, new seedlings in the ground. The plants were treated like living things, with dignity and respect for their purpose in life and their contribution to the community.

The airport was like a scar of concrete on the landscape, a necessary part of the conventional transportation system that tied the Eighth Day Village of the Sun to the outside world. Although not large, about the size of a small rural airport, the runway was long enough to accommodate giant transports and cargo planes. Far south of the village there was a seaport, the only other way to ship goods in and out of the area. The roads had long ago fallen into disrepair, unnecessary in a community with hovercraft and anti gravity devices, especially when most people preferred public transportation and walking.

A private plane sat on the runway, the pilot and plane surrounded by Eighth Day security. The passengers had already debarked and been cleared when Randall and the members of the Think Tank arrived. They were just now ambling through a gate making their way towards the Council. Baba Randall was the first to extend his hand, greeting T. Harmon Rothschild with a welcoming smile. The two shook hands as a flash jumped from Julie Ann Carver's camera.

"Please, please. No fuss.," said Randall.

"But this is a historic moment," said Julie. "Two men of power meeting to decide the world's fate."

"Julie Ann, how you cut words," said Rothschild, his voice deep and gruff. He was twice the size of Randall, his meaty frame tipping the scales at a cool three hundred. "I'm sorry. Randall, meet my publicist, Julie Ann Carver."

"Greetings," said Randall. "All of you. We've planned a little tour for you on our way to the hotel where I'm sure Julie Ann will find better things to photograph than two old men."

They all laughed, the nervous, forced laughter that is often heard when two diverse groups meet. They merged hesitantly, following formalities of handshakes and greetings reserved for visiting dignitaries. Talk began to fill the room with a soft murmur.

Sun Ki Han stared at Nan from across the room. He flashed a smile but she looked away, making small talk with Premier Kenji Alamoto. Fragments of conversation fell on his ears as Juliana came forward to greet him. As she reached for his hand, she felt something strange, a psychic vibration that made her frown. Sun ignored her, looking over her shoulder at Nan as she spoke with Alamoto. Juliana followed his gaze and seeing his lack of interest in her, moved on to greet Julie Ann Carver.

Nearby, Cardinal Jameson chatted casually with Darius. "So, how are you surviving this financial crisis?" he asked. "Did you lose everything in the stock market like most of us?"

"Fortunately our wealth is not tied to the markets," said Darius. "We trade in goods and services, precious metals, and knowledge. One of the goals of our community is have a sustainable economy. To achieve that, we trade first with each other, then with the outside."

"I see," said the Cardinal, a squint in his eye.

"Besides," said Darius. "The real wealth in any society is in its people."

Jameson smiled, adding a carefully spoken, "Yes. Of course."

Ravi and the General were also deep in conversation. "How do you deal with the thugs and gangs in Mexico?" asked Whiteweather.

"They know we are allies of a higher order," said Ravi. "They view us as a religious group, occasionally tithe and hire us for our services. They often use us as negotiators. We're known to be fair."

"Really?" asked the General, always interested on how to deal with hoodlums.

Ravi smiled. "That, and our Brujos keep them scared with little tricks. They're very superstitious."

Rothschild stayed close to Randall who introduced him to most of the members of the Think Tank. The fat man feigned interest, his real motives hidden so deep that even the High Priestess Juliana could not see into the darkness that surrounded him. As the crowd made their way through the exit doors and towards transportation, Van Dorn needled Singh, someone he had past dealings with.

"So, Singh. Still deciphering crop circles?" he asked.

Cameron's reply was succinct. "Still heating your home with oil,

Franklin?"

Once outside, Mel explained the transportation they were about to ride. "This tram moves by magnetic induction powered by solar panels. It's the first mass transit that we built. It will take us from the airport and over the mountains to the city."

"Charming," said Chase. "Seems I rode something like this at Disney World."

"I know," said Mel excitedly. "The people mover. Why didn't more of the world adopt that technology? Over a century of service and they're still actively operating in Tomorrowland."

They boarded the tram, some choosing open air cars over the coaches. Silently, the magnetic impulse engine engaged and they began an arduous, yet stunning path up and over the mountain. The tracks were raised, built on pillars that set it above the fields. Ahead lie the mountains, a thin line of rail along the rock face tracing the upward path they would soon follow.

"For security, the village is separated from the airport by these mountains," said Ravi.

"How do you move your air freight from the airport?" asked the General.

Antigravity was the true answer but instead Ravi said, "We have a special cargo train that we use. Runs along these same rails." Originally that was the truth. The village had started with such a system but after negotiations with the Galactics the cargo tram now only services people.

The tram moved up the mountain, the tracks following a narrow precipice with a view thousands of feet down into the valley. They rode past buildings built into the mountainside, updated versions of ancient cliff dwellings. The tram turned and entered a tunnel.

Lights came on and off as it passed through the darkness illuminating frescoes and artwork painted on the walls. It emerged into a cool mountain pass, nearby peaks reflected in a deep blue lake that lay beside the tracks. They traveled through fields of flowers, terraced farmland, and groves of high altitude crops. Animals were everywhere, mountain goats and fox, cougar and deer, monkeys and rabbits. Overhead, an eagle rode the wind. They passed a temple resting on a high mountaintop, man carved steps leading up to it. As they exited the mountain pass the village briefly came into view. The tram again hugged the mountainside as it wound down the side and toward the seacoast. They skirted the massive crystal mountain, the passengers gaping in awe at the rainbow of colors reflected from the many facets.

"I notice a lot of use of crystals in your architecture," said Chase. "Do you have a mine nearby?"

"No," said Mel. "We grow them."

"Grow them! Gads, man. They're as big as houses."

"Yes," said Mel. "You get the picture. We can grow them into the shapes of houses. Use them for refugees and potential settlers."

"What are they? Quartz?" asked Chase.

"Some of them," explained Mel. "Some are diamond. Some adamantine. We experiment with different crystals."

Chase was astounded. "Do you realize what would happen to the world economy if this ever got out? The diamond market would collapse. The DeBeers would go bankrupt overnight."

Ravi joined in. "Which is why we don't export them."

Darius could not restrain himself. "And look what happened anyway. The world went bankrupt without us."

33

"What are you trying to say Darius?" asked Rothschild.

"Simply that we thrive here because we don't own anything," he said.

"What do you mean, you're a Communist?" asked the General.

Darius drew a deep breath, his voice softening as if he were talking to children. "When you reach a higher state of mind you realize that everything, including life, is borrowed. Your desire for money fades and you find that you have everything you need for your purpose in life."

Chase sneered. "Right," he said indignantly.

Ravi explained. "Capitalism is not the only system to live by. As hard as you may find this to believe, there are people here living without money. They practice sustainability, grow enough food for their needs, trade with neighbors in work and food."

"Ah! Like the Amish," said the Cardinal.

"Yes," said Ravi agreeing. "Very similar."

"Here, we do not love money," said Darius. "We need it. We all have mundane jobs. We all work and provide for ourselves, trade in money at times. We use it to deal with communities and states beyond our borders. Some of the spiritual work we do cannot be done without money."

"You mean you collect money through your churches?" asked the Cardinal.

"No, said Darius. "We recognize, like many economists, that money flows like a river of electricity lighting every wallet. When the love of money is replaced by a love of humanity, you suddenly realize that people are the real wealth and the riches of the universe are at our disposal. There is enough here for everyone. There always has been."

"What if I want a mansion and can't afford one?" asked Chase. "Doesn't that lead to unhappiness? Discontent? Haves and have nots?"

Baba Randall laughed. "Let me tell you about Vera. A delightful woman! Very wise. She is a maid here. Works at the resort, maybe you'll get to meet her. She wanted a large house. Not having one made her unhappy. When Mel heard her story, he gave her his. A huge house on the hill overlooking the lagoon."

Rothschild looked at Mel in astonishment. "You gave her a house?!"

"No, I gave her her own mansion," said Mel. "Sure, the house gave me pleasure, but it didn't match the pleasure I got from watching her take ownership of it and fill it with her light, her love and energy."

Randall continued the story. "Eventually, she moved in. That energy grew until it filled every corner of that mansion with gratitude. Her heart softened and spread wide, opening outward with desire to serve others. Then she learned a valuable lesson. Sometime when we own things, they own us. She loved the house, but spent a lot of time cleaning it and fixing it. She worked all the time, cleaning other people's things and then coming home to clean her own. After some time, she realized the truth, that things own us. Not long after that she moved out and thanked Mel for letting her borrow the mansion, realizing that he gave her the greatest gift of all: the opportunity to learn and advance spiritually."

"Well, Mel, at least you got your mansion back," said Rothschild. "If you still don't want it, I'll be glad to take it off your hands."

Mel stared at him. "And what would you learn from that?" There was a silence, after which Mel nodded. "Uh-huh."

Randall noticed the awkwardness and moved the conversation on. "Speaking about houses, tomorrow we will tour an empty refugee camp where we grew a field of homes. Some structures were constructed of native material, rock, rammed earth, and aircrete. Most of these are central buildings like the community kitchens, meeting halls, waste processing centers, greenhouses, and such. Naturally we will show you how to create these centers so you can help your people form communities and hasten their recovery."

The tour continued, a last opportunity to show more of Eighth Day Village of the Sun. They passed what looked like a grocery store attached to an open air market. A sign overhead read "FOOD BANK". They passed a manufactory, a series of buildings on site labeled "ENERGY CENTER", "RECYCLE", "SCRAP", and "WAREHOUSE". A man operating a forklift moved pallets of material in the courtyard outside, happy in his work. He waved at them with a wide smile on his face as the tram rolled by. The hotels and resorts they passed were opulent, beyond anything seen at the world's best destinations. Eventually the tram came to a stop at the bottom of the mountain where they disembarked.

Ravi pulled them together. "This part of the tour includes a walk through our public gardens. Look around. Feel free to pick and eat any fruit or vegetables you see. There are compost bins throughout the grounds, well marked."

"I'd love to get a closer look at that power plant we just passed," said Rothschild.

"Sorry, that's restricted," said Darius. "Not part of the tour."

"Not even for me?" asked Rothschild.

"There are no exceptions," said Baba Randall. "Even I abide by our security standards. But let me show you something else you might find interesting. Our historical society has a small museum where you'll find a lot of your questions answered. It's right over here."

The tourguide speech faded and the bulk of the group moved on, their focus ahead rather than behind them. In a swift motion, Sun grabbed Nan and pulled her aside, pushing her into a nearby alcove.

It was an idyllic setting, rich with flowers and a white leopard sitting peacefully on a rock across a pond behind them. Nearby a fountain sprayed a canopy of water over a soft stone structure. Birds abounded, their chirping a song to their ears. Sun saw none of this. He held her tightly by the shoulders, looking into her eyes with ravenous hunger. "Did you miss me, Nan?" he asked.

She looked hesitantly at his grip on her shoulders, her head moving from side to side. He got the message and let go. She composed herself before speaking. "For a long time I missed you," she said. "There were times I cried. I came to understand the source of my grief."

"What does that mean? I don't understand."

"It means I'm over you," said Nan. "I've moved on. I found I don't need a man around all the time to be satisfied with my life."

"Really?" he asked, surprised at her answer. He looked over her shoulder at the fountain and smiled. "Is that one of your village's famous sex fountains?"

She turned and looked, even though she knew it was. "Yes."

He looked at her and nodded. "You want to have a go at it?" He drooled at the thought. "It's okay to have public sex in these things, or so I hear."

"As I said, Sun. I'm finished with you. We had our time."

"It was a good time, yeah?" There was desperation in his voice, his eyes held haunted memories of a relationship gone sour.
She did not answer, instead looked off, staring over his shoulder. She nodded her head sadly.

He turned to where she had been staring. "You still talking to invisible people?" he asked.

"If you mean, am I in contact with my angelic team and higher dimensional beings, then, yes," she said.

Sun laughed, twisting her words in his head. "Invisible people. I've always had a thing for crazy women. You still want to breed and have a family?" He nodded towards the sex fountain again.

Nan shook her head. "I'm sad for you, Sun. You'll never understand how rich life can be, even without fame and fortune."

"Yeah? Well look at me now, Nan," he said, arrogance filling his voice. "I'm traveling with Morgan Rothschild at his invitation. My input on this team is valued. If you play ball with me, you could be a part of this."

"Sorry, Sun," she said. "I'm already a part of a team that values my input."

She went to step around him and leave the alcove. In a sudden move, he grabbed her by the shoulders again and kissed her. She pulled away, looking at him in disgust. Behind them the white leopard roared and stood up, alert and ready to pounce. Nan turned and spoke to her in a gentle voice. "It's okay, Leah. He meant no harm. I know this kind of animal behavior upsets you, but he meant no harm."

Leah roared again. Nan walked over and pet the leopard, turning back to Sun. "You better leave. Rejoin the tour. I'd hate to see you miss it because you were mauled for your stupidity."

Sun bit his lower lip, stared at them both for a moment, afraid to move. In a grand gesture, he turned and left quickly. Nan continued to pet the leopard. "Yes, poor fool. He doesn't know you're just a kitten."

Leah roared, then purred, her eyes squinting in pleasure as Nan continued to stroke her gently. She hugged the white leopard one more time before ducking away to follow the tour route and catch up with the group.

5

Sun managed to get lost, wandering in the gardens until he finally admitted he had no way of finding his way back. He was about to give up, sit down on a nearby bench and scream in frustration. An old man stopped and recognized him. "You're Sun Ki Han," he said.

"My fame proceeds me," said Sun.

The meaning was lost on the old man. "I recognize you from the morning teleconference with the Think Tank."

That meaning was lost on Sun. He drew a deep breath. "I'm lost," he said. "I was following a tour when I... I saw something interesting and stopped to investigate."

The old man looked at him and nodded gravely. "You're lost all right. In more ways than one," he said. "Keep the truth to yourself. Hide it from me. Just be careful you don't hide it from yourself. After all, you have to live with it."

Sun shook his head, squinted his eyes. "What!" he said in disbelief. "Look, just help me find my way back to my tour."

The old man walked over to a crystal, a dominant feature in a nearby alcove. He closed his eyes and laid his hands on the giant piece of quartz. A nearby wall lit up, light projecting from the heart of the stone. It displayed a map, the path of the tour clearly marked along with their present location. "It's right around the corner," he said to Sun, pointing the direction. "Listen! I can almost hear them talking."

Sun turned walked a short distance where he heard Chase talking about the animals. He turned to thank the old man but he was gone. True to his words, though, the group was just around the corner.

"I've never seen so many exotic animals in an uncaged environment," said Chase. "Your investment in them must be significant. The peacocks alone must be worth, what, fifty thousand?"

"I'm sorry," said Baba Randall. "I thought you understood. This is not a zoo. We don't own the animals. They are as free as the giraffes in Mexico."

"But you feed them," said Van Dorn.

"And they are grateful for that," said Randall. "And they also appreciate us. We form a personal relationship that way, especially if we don't eat them."

"Do they ever want to eat you?" asked Sun.

"There's the game," said Randall. "If you are one with nature, you are one with the animals. And what sane creature, one with nature, would destroy itself?"

Singh added a comment. "In ancient Egyptian times people controlled animals through thought. There was psychic communication and telepathy between man and animals. You often see it pictured in hieroglyphics. Not all people, but high beings often kept the company of lions and tigers. If they faltered from their spirituality or lost their oneness with the Universe, the animal would graciously eat them."

"Graciously," commented the General.

Sun was about to say something about his recent encounter when Randall chimed in.

"Well, thank you for that history lesson, Cameron," he said. "And now I think we have a ride planned for us in solar powered cars. Mel, would you be so good as to explain."

Mel took the cue, "We started with golf cart sized cars. They were easy to solarize. We simply embedded the roof with solar panels and installed lightweight batteries. We did a lot of experimentation with other forms of energy storage including flywheels, springs, and crystals. This all led to the creation of the hybrid cars we will ride in today."

"Hybrid?" asked Rothschild. "Are they gas powered too?"

"We don't use petroleum here for propulsion," said Mel. "A hybrid also uses gravometric propulsion."

"What's that?" asked Van Dorn. "I never heard of that."

"It's been around for a while," said Mel. "The Earth is a giant magnet, emitting lines of magnetic force running from pole to pole. Birds often follow these lines in their migration paths. We simply mapped these lines and developed a device that could take advantage of the different energy levels between the lines."

"What do you mean?" asked Rothschild. "I still don't get it."

"Let me explain simply," said Mel. "Thermal energy takes advantage of the difference in temperature between two things. Atomic, the energy differences of certain fissionable material. Hydroelectric, the action of gravity between two different levels of water. In the course of the water falling, the energy is captured through a turbine and used to generate electricity. Similarly, the gravity lines have different levels of magnetic energy."

"A new energy source? How much do these things cost?" asked Van Dorn.

Randall interrupted his train of thought. "Shhh! Listen!"

"What?" said Van Dorn. "I don't hear anything."

"Precisely," said Randall. "The birds have stopped chirping. The animals are silent."

There was a blaring sound. A wailing of sirens.

"What's that?" asked Chase.

"Sounds like an old time air raid siren," said the General.

"The emergency signal," said Randall. "We'd better get to the bunker. It's not far. We'll walk, but quickly. This way please. Follow Ravi."

They passed throngs of people moving through the streets and passageways towards some unknown destination. Ravi cut left, away from the crowd and towards a low, flat building marked with a sign reading "Control Room." The doors were thick, heavy metal that looked like it could withstand a nuclear blast.

"Bet they didn't plan this as part of the tour," said the General.

Inside the Control Room there was a flurry of activity. Ravi led them past desks and alcoves staffed with people focused on their tasks. Some pored over reports, some stared intently into computer screens, others wore microphones and headsets, intense conversations adding to the drama. They passed desk areas marked with overhead hanging signs: "ENERGY", "PLANNING", "MITIGATION", "EMERGENCY SERVICES", "LOGISTICS".

"This is an emergency operations center," said the General.

"Yes," said Ravi. "Good show, General."

"Where are we going?"

"Right over here," said Ravi. "Take a seat."

They passed a small conference table in the back of the room. Dr. Darius, Barclay, and Mel joined the people seated there. Juliana sat quietly beside them and closed her eyes entering into a deep trance. Wall mounted monitors around them displayed data, nearby analysts calculating and making predictions. Ravi led the rest to several rows of theater seating where the visiting dignitaries nervously settled down. It gave them a balcony view of the entire operation.

"What's going on?" asked Rothschild.

"I'm not sure," said Van Dorn.

"We should sit quietly and observe," said the General. "This seems to be their show."

Randall sat in a special seat off to the side, a raised platform with a padded chair. Below him, Darius spoke with several people before turning and approaching him. "Baba Randall. We have an emergency."

"So I take it," said Randall. "I haven't lost my hearing yet. Mel's early warning system is working fine. And our drills worked. Everyone in the village is safely at their station. What's the situation?"

"Our early warning system has detected a tsunami headed directly for our city," said Darius.

"A tsunami," said Randall. "How fortunate!"

Sun stood up. "What? Are you insane? We should be evacuating to high ground."

"He's right. This building is too close to the shore for protection," said Cardinal Jameson.

Randall smiled and calmly turned away from them. "What is the mean predicted wave height, Dr. Darius?"

"Five hundred meters," said Darius.

"Fools!" said Sun. "We'll all be killed." He got up from his seat, pushed his way toward the aisle where he was intercepted by a Guard.

Darius nodded. "Patience, Sun Ki. Give us a chance. Take a seat and be calm like the rest of us."

"Five hundred meters," said Rothschild. "Don't you think we should be heading up the mountain right now?"

"No time," said Ravi. "Five hundred meters is a pretty big tsunami, but we're seeing more and more this size since global warming took full effect. We've dealt with them before, and we wouldn't have built our village in a hazard zone without proper emergency procedures. Trust us. We want to survive as much as you do."

Juliana's eyes opened, awakening calm from her meditation. "I have spoken with Gaia," she said. "A rupture in the Japanese Islands has caused an earthquake. Underwater mining operations have opened a fissure near the Median Tectonic Line."

A technician verified her statement. "Data confirmed. Tsunami origin east of Fukushima."

"Tell Gaia we are sorry," said Randall. "Assemble the Group Meditation circle. Have them focus on love and healing. Pray for our safety."

"Already done, Baba," said Juliana. "The group met at the first blast of the horn. They love Mother Earth as much as I do. Or anybody else in this room." She glared at Sun. "Well, not quite everybody."

"That's enough, Juliana," said Randall.

"What?" she said. "Turn the other cheek? Look what it's got you, Baba."

Randall looked about the emergency center, his hands wide with admiration as he smiled. "Yes, look at what it got us."

The technician interrupted. "Wave approaching, sir. One hundred kilometers and coming in fast."

"Have you completed your calculations, Darius?" asked Randall.

"Yes. We've calculated the wavelength and are ready to match resonance." He turned to the technician and gave the command. "Deploy the LRAD."

"LRAD?" said the General. "A Long Range Acoustical Device?"

"Precisely," said Ravi. "The same thing you use to dispel an angry mob in your world, General."

Outside on the roof of the operations center, a barrel shaped device with a dish antenna at one end appeared out of a box. It elevated and pointed seaward towards the lagoon.

"LRAD deployed and ready," said the technician.

Darius gave the order. "Commence operations."

"Activating LRAD," said the technician.

There was a low bass sound, an acoustical wave of energy aimed at the approaching tsunami.

"The wave is subsiding, Doctor," said the technician.

"Prepare to harness the energy," replied Darius.

The tsunami approached the city with a vengeance, all five hundred meters of it. The water in the lagoon of the Eighth Day Village of the Sun drained, a sign the tsunami was close. Boats were grounded, coral reefs exposed, and fish left flapping in panic on the clean white sand. The LRAD aimed at the exposed sand causing it to shiver with the power of the bass sound. As the wave passed over the sand, it began to tremble and shake, suddenly turning into rain.

Darius gave another order. "Open the salt water cisterns."

Water poured into the open vents, filling to capacity. The overflow raced down a turbine shaft, rotating a coil that electrostatically charged a dynamo.

"The molecular spring is at capacity, Sir," reported the technician.

"Okay," said Darius. "Cut power. Open the storm drains. Divert all water back to the sea."

A light rain fell over the village. A mist passed over the farmland of terraced crops against the hillside. Streams surged with life and on a mountain behind the city a waterfall burst with newfound energy. The lagoon filled again, fed by rivulets of water washing the land fresh. There was no damage. On the beach, not even an umbrella was tipped, the chairs resting gently beneath them. At Manny's beachside bar, the drinks he abandoned during the emergency were waiting to be completed, the barstools upright and ready to be occupied. At a nearby table, light rain fell on a pineapple shaped glass covered with a paper umbrella.

Darius went over to Randall. "Our systems are fully charged, and it looks like Lake Quetzalcoatl is filled to capacity."

Juliana raised her arms. "Thank you Gaia."

"Yes, thank you Gaia," said Baba Randall.

They all bowed their heads, everyone in the operations center, even a few of the visitors, but not Sun, Rothschild, or Chase. Baba Randall noticed this. "It's sad you don't see it," he said.

"See what, Randall?" asked Sun.

"Whether you recognize it or not, you have a relationship with Mother Earth," said Randall.

"Mother Earth just tried to destroy us," said Sun. "Look what she's done to Hawaii. Volcanoes in Wyoming? For Christ's sake, man, Washington DC is below sea level. The levee gets higher and more expensive every year."

"You brought this on yourself," said Juliana.

"Come, come," said Randall, ever the peacemaker. "Let's not debate how we got here. Let's talk about the solution."

"Yes, yes," said Cardinal Jameson. "That's why we are all here. A solution."

"Is that so, Cardinal Jameson?" said Barclay. "No member of your party has actually stated why they are here and what they want from us."

Chase chimed in. "Isn't it obvious? We need your help. With a loan from you to the International Monetary Fund of, say, twenty billion..."

Rothschild interrupted him. "That's enough, Rockefeller," he said.

There was a pregnant pause, as if someone had made a terrible faux pas and had no way to correct it. The monitors in the room showed news feeds of the world's turmoil. Riots, hunger, suffering, the pain of humanity displayed on multiple television screens mounted on the walls. Randall was compassionately drawn to these powerful images while the silence reigned. From his dais he pointed them out with his eyes and a nod of his head for all to witness.

"Sorry," said Chase.

"The event is over, sir," said the technician. "We can sound all clear. Eighth Day Village of the Sun is safe." After a pause he added. "I can't say the same for the rest of the world. Sir."

They stared at the monitors, painful images in the background. The tension of leaders filled the foreground, clenched fists, tightened jaws, glaring eyes. The all clear siren sounded, the images slowly replaced with camera views of the Eighth Day Village of the Sun. One large screen cycled through images of New Maya City of Worlds. The tension seemed to fade as the General unclenched his fists, Sun assumed a more relaxed posture, and Chase looked down at the floor, moving aside and out of the limelight.

"I think we've had enough excitement for the day, Randall," said Rothschild. "Can we cut the rest of the tour short and settle in at our hotel?"

"Of course, Harmon. How about we meet again at dinner tonight?"

asked Randall.

"Perhaps," said Rothschild. "Right now I'm fatigued and need to rest."

Randall called to his faithful aide. "Ravi? Could you see that our guests get to their rooms?"

6

The Grand Suite at the Reiki Spa and Resort was an exercise in opulence. Patterned after the exorbitant resorts built by the Sheikhs, it lacked for nothing. Harmon Rothschild poured himself a drink and dismissed the servants for the night. He stared out at the lagoon, an impressive view from the balcony of his suite. There was a knock at the door. He opened it and greeted Chase, Kenji, and the General.

"Well, was that dinner the most elaborate feast of fruit and vegetables you ever saw?" he asked.

"I was never a fan of vegetables," said Chase. "I like meat. They don't eat much meat here."

"The fish was good," commented Kenji.

"The food agreed with me," said General Whiteweather. "I feel contented, like you should after a fine meal."

Chase sneered. "Anything is better than what they feed you in the army."

"How would you know, Chase," said the General. "You never saw a day of military service in your life."

"I don't get it" said Rothschild, closing the door behind them. "A five star restaurant without a cut of meat on the menu. But enough about the bad dinner, let's get down to business."

Rothschild directed them towards the balcony where he and Kenji stepped out. The General took a small, square device out of his pocket and activated it. Meanwhile, Chase swept the room with a miniature hand held scanner paying close attention to the flickering lights on the device, stopping and repeating his sweep occasionally. Finally they were both done. They nodded to each other and joined Morgan and Kenji on the balcony. The General placed his square device on the low table between them as they took seats and repositioned deck chairs for more comfort.

"Jamming frequency at full power," reported the General. "They can't eavesdrop on our conversation."

"No cameras or recording devices in the room or in range," said Chase.

"Where is Van Dorn?" asked Rothschild.

"He's trying to sneak into one of their power plants and take a peek," said Chase. "He's been trying to figure out how they supply enough energy to power most of Mexico and Central America. They even sell to California now, and it's cheap. We figured, given their investment against the output, it can't be solar or wind based, and it's certainly not petroleum based."

"Could that tsunami really provide enough energy to power everything?" asked the General. "I wouldn't think so. They don't occur that frequently."

"They said they charged some kind of molecular spring," said Chase.

"What is that?" asked Kenji. "A water based spring or a mechanical spring?"

Rothschild sighed. "We'll let Van Dorn worry about it. If he cracks that egg we're back on top. Energy has always been a significant source of wealth and a point of control." He took a sip of his drink and settled back in his chair, satisfied. "Well, here we are boys. I didn't think we'd get this far. We're Jonah, inside the belly of the whale."

"It was easy," said Chase. "They're so trusting."

Rothschild snickered. "They really want to save the Earth, save humanity."

"Did you see their refugee center?" asked the General. "Like we're going to take a bunch a seeds back and grow a village."

"Or crystals," said Kenji. "Actually, the idea is quite intriguing. It could really benefit my people."

Rothschild frowned. "Don't get taken in and go soft on us, Alamoto."

"I wonder how much value we would put on a crystal house," said Chase. "Would the mortgage be affordable?"

"What mortgage?" said Rothschild. "Didn't you hear the dinner conversation? They want to give houses away free. Next thing you know they'll be giving away food!"

"They do already," said Kenji. "Nobody pays for food in this village. They make free withdrawals from the food bank. There's a mountain around here honeycombed with caves where they store excess production. Grains, dried fruits, and vegetable extracts. They estimate there's enough food stored to feed the world for six months or more."

"Nan was telling Kenji and I their plan," said Chase. "They want to teach permaculture, vertical gardening, and aquaponics. As part of the training they build gardens and leave them behind."

"Too many of these small gardens could offset the control we have on the centralized food industry."

Rothschild sneered. "We lose the seed business, the supermarket dollar, the land value. "

"Petroleum based agricultural products, too," added Kenji. "Did you know they don't use fertilizer or pesticides?"

"What do they use?" asked General Whiteweather.

"Fish and seaweed fertilizer," said Kenji.

"They must get low yields," said Rothschild.

"Actually, higher than average," explained Kenji. "They compost and use manure, manage pests by growing certain things like marigolds and garlic side by side with food crops. They use soap sprays, beneficial organisms, and EM."

"EM? What's that?" asked Rothschild.

"Effective microorganisms," said Kenji. "Tiny bugs that improve the soil and promote healthy plant life."

"I've heard of such practices," said Chase.

"Yes. Just like my great, great grandfather," said the General. "It sets agriculture back a hundred years or more."

"No, I believe it takes agriculture two hundred years forward," said Alamoto.

"What do you mean, Kenji?" asked Rothschild.

"It's labor intensive, but it puts love and energy into the food," he said. "They establish personal relations with the plants." He chuckled. "It's an interesting practice, kind of quaint."

"Damn it, man. It threatens everything we worked for," said Rothschild. "We have to put a stop to it before these people act out their crazy plan."

"They're eager," said Kenji. "They'd start tomorrow if we'd let them."

Rothschild cleared his throat. "What was the death toll today?"

"Media estimates it was close to seventeen million," said Chase.

Rothschild pondered it for a moment. "Seventeen million! Imagine that. We tightened the food supply two weeks ago. Stores must be empty by now. Three, maybe four more days we'll lose a hundred million. What do you think?"

"Hundred million easy," said Chase.

"And if we delay a week a few hundred million more," said Rothschild.

The General's eyes widened. Loss of life, whether in combat or by civilian means, always remained his main concern. "What's your point?" he asked.

Kenji narrowed his eyes, sensing the discomfort in the General. Rothschild didn't notice. He was deep in thought. "This may work to our advantage. A smaller population is easier to control."

Kenji felt the discomfort now. He cast a sideways glance at the General. Chase was enthralled. He leaned forward in his chair hanging on Rothschild's words.

Two empty chairs lay nearby, silent sentinels of sanity, unnoticed as Rothschild continued to talk about domination and control of the world's population. But the chairs were not empty. The astral forms of Juliana and Cameron Singh sat patiently listening to everything that was being said. From their advantage they saw more than one could with eyes. Juliana heard words that came from their hearts, often different than what was said. Singh interpreted the malformed stains he observed in their auras, but even with all his abilities, Rothschild remained hidden in darkness. He nodded to Juliana, his astral heart bleeding with pain.

There was a whooshing sound. Juliana opened her eyes back in her room, awakening as fresh as she would through meditation.

"Oh my God," she said out loud. "Darius was right! I have to warn him."

7

It was late in the evening, not the usual time for a meeting of the Think Tank, yet some of the members assembled to discuss the situation. Baba Randall and Ravi were conspicuously absent, their chairs empty. The room was lit low, conspiratorial. Around the table sat Nan, Darius, Stine, Barclay, and Mel.

"I told you what Cameron and I saw," said Juliana. "Singh is monitoring the situation. Otherwise he would be here."

The astral form of Cameron Singh appeared in an empty chair.

"Actually, I am here," he said.

"Then who's keeping an eye on our friends?" asked Darius.

"Actually, I am," said Singh. "I can be in two places at once, easy enough for a ninth dimensional Atlantean."

"Thank you Cameron," said Darius.

"Why isn't Randall here?" asked Barclay.

"I'll brief him in the morning," said Darius. "Let's monitor the problem for now. Meanwhile, anyone have any ideas on how to deal with this?"

"We can't let millions of innocent people die, especially when we have the resources to feed them," said Nan.

"I agree," said Juliana.

"I contacted New Maya City of Worlds earlier today," said Barclay. "Our sister community has excess production to share. Plenty of food. They also ramped up their clothing manufactories and expanded their line to include more blankets and camping gear."

"Excellent," said Mel. "Let them know we're available if they need more manpower."

"I like their stuff," said Juliana. "Comfortable, made of natural fibers harvested from the jungle."

"Okay, so we have the resources," said Darius. "That still doesn't solve our problem. How do we move past these lower dimensional beings that are in control?"

"We could have the Galactics shut the whole thing down," suggested Singh.

"Let's see if we can solve it ourselves, Cameron," said Darius. "The aliens like it better when we work that way."

"That's good for a last resort, though," suggested Barclay.

"The Galactics have their hands full keeping the dark aliens at bay," said Mel. "The Darks cause most of the trouble in the world to begin with."

"I thought we had a peace treaty with the dark aliens," said Barclay.

"We did," said Singh. "The treaty stated that the Earth would be allowed to hold both Light and Dark forces until the time when Gaia would be allowed to evolve and begin her ascension into higher realms. That time is now. The Darks were supposed to leave the planet by now but they haven't."

"This must be their last gambit," said Barclay. "World chaos. Why haven't the governments disclosed that we've known about extraterrestrial life for some time now?"

"Look. I agree with Darius," said Mel. "Let's keep the aliens out of this for now. We can solve our own problems."

"How about this?" said Juliana. "We put a hex on them."

Nan was shocked. "Juliana! What next, kill them?"

Singh perked up at her comment. "And take control of the time line? Interesting solution, one often debated when talking about Hitler."

"Now, now. Get off this track," said Darius. "No one is going to break the Universal Law."

"I'm not talking about murder," said Juliana. "Just a little hex."

"What you suggest would not help," said Stine. "Evil cannot be conquered in the world, only resisted from within. These people represent a mass conglomerate bent on controlling humanity for their own comfort. We have to come up with a better way."

"True, true," said Darius. "What about a non-violent solution then?"

"Yes! It's what Randall would require anyway," said Stine.

"Quiet for a moment," said Juliana. "Let's put our energies together. Invoke help from our angelic team and the light workers around us. The solution is at hand."

They nodded in agreement and closed their eyes to meditate together. In their minds, flashes of insight illuminated the future without revealing too much detail. Cameron saw the world's population being fed. Juliana sensed that the General was upset with Rothschild. He seemed to care. Nan had inner knowledge that Kenji Alamoto was not really part of this group, that he had invited himself to this party in the hope of finding a solution for his people. His main concern was the fate of Africa, a land racked by colonialism. The outside world always sought to control their precious resources. Diamonds, gold, ivory, and food, these were the activities that made up life for his people. Above all, Kenji wanted them free of Western influence, in control of their own destiny, a self sustaining continent where there was enough for everybody.

Rothschild definitely stood between the Village and success. Van Dorn and Chase were unknowns. It was obvious that Julie Ann Carver was not part of this group, but could she be counted on when needed?

These thoughts swirled in their heads, telepathically shared in group meditation. It was the power of the Think Tank, the ability to share consciousness and focus on spiritual solutions.

After a short time, they slowly opened their eyes, a smile and a knowing glance across their faces.

"Yes," said Darius. "The solution was obvious. Let's get to it then. Nan, you focus on Kenji Alamoto."

Nan turned quickly. "Just what are you suggesting, Darius? That I use feminine wiles and deceit to achieve our ends?"

"The fate of the world is at hand," said Darius.

"Deceit is not necessary," said Cameron, his voice cool and knowledgeable. "Are you denying that fire is not burning already?"

Nan looked down and into herself, a pregnant pause in the air as the group looked on. After a moment she responded, "He is a true humanitarian, humble and appreciative of what we have here." Her eyes closed, as if she were sipping a rare tea, and added. "I can't help myself."

"Why not see where it leads?" said Singh. "Love is the grand adventure, good for the soul."

"Well," insisted Juliana, her energy taking the stage, "I have no issues with my femininity. This isn't about *wiles*, as you say. It's just good old fashioned, natural behavior to me."

Nan looked up and grew half a smile as if Juliana had poked her playfully.

"Sure. I'll take the General," said Juliana. "He interests me. He's powerful, and quite clear on the mental plane. He responds to logic. He's my kind of man."

"Every man is your kind of man, Juliana," said Barclay.

She smiled at him, slowly, seductively. "I am a Tantric Goddess like Nan. I welcome an honorable opportunity to practice the art." She turned towards Nan. "How about you?"

Nan once again looked inward, this time her face beginning to revel with her growing electricity.

Barclay smiled, enjoying the high priestess. Secretly he couldn't help wishing Juliana would practice with him.

"Good," said Darius. "You know what to do, then." He turned towards Dr. McKenner. "Barclay, what do you think about letting Van Dorn see our technology, except we..."

The secret meeting continued into the night.

8

Like all days, the sun rose over the Eighth Day Village of the Sun and lit the world with Light. The solar collectors were quickly at capacity, harnessing the ultimate source of all energy on the planet. The sun drove the winds, gave life to plants, and warmed the Earth. The beach gradually filled with sun worshipers, Randall included, trotting his giraffe between the small groups of sunbathers, yoga practitioners, and even a few young children building a sand castle.

By mid morning the tour was underway again. The group strolled through gardens, admiring buildings that fit in so well, they were almost invisible in the landscape. Birds chirped, wild animals abounded, running water and gentle breezes soothed the spirit. As they walked, groups eagerly discussed things they had seen on the tour. This is what was possible when community planning took into account more than just the people and land use. There were normal considerations like all cities, sustainable water practices, sewage processing, garbage disposal, and the like. The Village seemed to solve these problems by fostering the creative process among the citizens and allowing them to experiment. The results spoke for themselves.

Kenji talked with Nan about the agricultural fields they had just toured, a subject of interest since two thirds of Africa's population were engaged in agriculture and food production.

"I wouldn't have believed the yields you are getting on your crops if I hadn't seen it myself," he said. "Your gardens are impressive."

"You've only seen our community gardens where we grow small amounts for neighborhood use," said Nan. "I'd like to take you out to our fields and show you how we really do it."

Her knowledge of agriculture was extensive. He was attracted to her as much for her brain as her body. She exuded femininity, and Kenji could not resist smiling. "I would like that very much," he said. "And you say you can offer this to my people for free? Teach them to grow their own food?"

"Not just enough for themselves, but ten times that," she said. "We can also show you how to preserve it. Each person would become a super-producer. That frees people and resources for other things."

"Like growing houses?" said Kenji.

"Well, yes, but I can think of other things," said Nan. "Meditation, worship, giving thanks. Do you say grace and bless your food before you eat it?"

"Sometimes, not always."

"You should," said Nan. "There's a reason we say grace. I know people that live in places where, by necessity, they eat processed food, meat, and flavorless, mass produced vegetables. They tell me you can eat anything, and as long as you bless it, your body will absorb the best part and you will remain healthy."

"Interesting theory," said Kenji. "I can't help but think how this could benefit my people. Africa is a poor continent, and we have always struggled to provide enough. What you offer is beyond belief. I can't help but ask, why would you be so generous?"

Nan smiled and gently took his arm, wrapping hers around it. "Silly," she said. "Because it's the right thing to do."

They drew close, her arm locked in his. Behind them and slightly out of sight, Sun Ki Han, her ex-husband, glared at their backs.

Nearby, Randall was in deep conversation with Rothschild. "I don't know if money will solve your problems," he said.

"Money solves all problems," snorted Rothschild.

"I disagree," said Randall. "Money causes more problems than it solves."

Rothschild was taken aback. "Gads, man. Governments are failing. Give us the money to prop them up at least. What's going to happen when they crumble?"

Baba Randall looked off into space. "I had a dream about that once. All governments gone. A world where everyone governs themselves."

"Lawlessness," said Rothschild.

"Perhaps," said Randall. "Maybe for a short time, but I'd like to believe that people have a stronger moral compass than their present government. I would certainly trust my own judgment over some elected officials."

"In your world vision, how would we complete big projects? Roads and bridges, public monuments, national parks?"

Randall explained. "Same way we do here. We establish conscious, decision making committees drawn from the community's population. They meet and manage the project, wisely spend the little bit of money we allocate. They solve resource problems, create work schedules, and enjoy the process. The tram from the airport was built that way. Citizens formed a workgroup. Mel acted as chief engineer and talents were divided according to what tasks

64

best suited people."

Rothschild was amazed. "You have bridge builders, concrete experts, welders and laborers on hand?"

Randall elaborated. "And zookeepers, schoolteachers, blacksmiths, laser physicists, babysitters. Anyone who wants to get involved. We run training camps for those who want to learn."

"How did you pay for it?" asked Rothschild. "Municipal bonds?"

"Not needed," said Randall. "We absorbed some cost of materials, but it was all volunteer labor."

"That's crazy," said Rothschild.

"Is it?" said Randall. "The community realized a need for it, and people stepped up to the task. It was a thing to see. A wave of energy took over as more and more citizens got involved. It was completed in half the time just because of the level of involvement."

"They didn't demand wages?" asked Rothschild. "Strike for better working conditions?"

"We don't get many complaints in the Eighth Day Village of the Sun," said Randall. "People here take care of themselves, and each other. As for wages, what would they spend it on? We provide free food and entertainment, transportation, housing. The tram is free because the effort made by the community is a sunk cost."

"Somebody has to pay for it eventually," said Rothschild. "The manufacturer, the service provider. Someone."

"And they do," said Randall. "Each of us contributes their labor. We pay for it in work. We ask for nothing in return and instead get everything."

"Kind of like a one price, overgrown Caribbean resort," said Rothschild.

Randall laughed at the comparison. "Yes! Except the villagers are on vacation as well as the guests. If you would just embrace the world rather than trying to control it, Rothschild, you would see there's enough for everyone. Can you at least think of a world where everyone is a *have* and there are no *have-nots*?"

"What would happen to all my stuff?" asked Rothschild. "My yachts and mansions?"

"Oh, you'd still have it all," said Randall. "Nobody else wants it, Rothschild. Your vision of society creates the need for these things, ours eliminates it. I see you've already forgotten my story about Vera the maid. If you were enlightened, you would know this."

Darius was slightly behind them talking to Chase. "Do you remember me, Chase?" he asked.

"Vaguely," he said. He was more interested in studying the Village than listening to Darius go on about something else.

"You were in charge of Corporate Loans for you bank," said Darius. "The highest authority. Randall and I came to you for help, must have been thirty or forty years ago."

Chase tried to remember. "Really?" he said.

"Despite being over capitalized and over collateralized, you turned us down, remember?"

"Did I?" said Chase. "I must have had a good reason."

"Whatever it was, I have to thank you," said Darius. "Had we accepted that loan we'd probably still be paying the interest on it.

66

As it stands we're debt free and bursting with a healthy surplus."

Chase retorted snidely. "What a miracle," he snorted.

Darius was calm, smiling. "No miracle, just a change in tact. Instead of loans we got grants from some of the wealthiest people in the world. Mostly internet millionaires who believed in our vision. Some of them live here now."

"Grants," said Chase. "You don't have to pay those back. How lucky for you."

"Not as lucky as we were when we used crowdsourcing to fund the rest," said Darius.

"Oh, you mean those cheesy web sites like kickstarter, go fund me, and speculate?" said Chase. "And what kind of quaint offering did you give your investors?"

"A place in this community," said Darius. "If they wanted it, of course. Or free vacations for life, depending on their level of contribution. We had five buildings and then all of a sudden twenty million people signed up donating over 300 million to get us started. Many of them came to live here and work with us. Many of them just came for the vacations and spent more money." He gently clapped Chase on the back. "Anyway, just wanted to thank you. In a way, we couldn't have done it without you."

Chase looked down at the ground, chastened, a frown etched on his face.

Darius continued. "Oh, and if you're looking for us to loan your bank some money, well, yeah, we don't do that. Loan money, I mean. But hey, you might want to think about crowdsourcing. I'm sure there's twenty million people out there who believe just as strongly in your bank as they did in Eighth Day Village of the Sun."

The tour group came to a stop, assembled in front of a small, low building.

"We have arrived at the hospital," said Ravi.

"You mean the doctor's office," said the General. "This is hardly a hospital."

"I assure you General. This is our one and only hospital," said Ravi. "Does anyone need medical assistance? The green light is on and you can go in."

"I'd like to give it a try," said Van Dorn.

Julie Ann Carver perked up, too. "And if you don't mind, I could use a second opinion about something."

"One at a time please," said Randall. "Franklin, why don't you go first."

Van Dorn tried to open the door but it was locked. Randall saw the problem immediately and went over to the door. He gently moved him aside. "Sorry," he said. "Like all our resources, the hospital is for community members only, but we can make exceptions." He spoke into a speaker by the door. "Admit non community member. Emergency override Randall 1, Authorization 1, Code 1-1A."
The door opened easily and Van Dorn entered.

Chase made a comment. "You must have run out of money when you got to this project. What's the matter? The community wanted to build a tram but not a hospital?"

"We build what we need, Chase," said Randall. "We have birthing centers which are a bit more elaborate, but this is all we need as far as medicine. The focus in our community is on wellness."

"Surely, you have medical doctors?" asked Rothschild.

"On call if needed," said Randall. "Most of them have retired from practice to focus on research. Some deal with patients, but they are not very busy."

"What about surgeries?" asked Rothschild. "Procedures? Examination instruments?"

"We have none of that," said Randall. "Our approach to procedures and surgery are quite different from traditional Western medicine. Even instrumentation. We have found cheaper and less harmful ways to probe the human body."

Ravi chimed in. "We are not ruled by the A.M.A. Here, we embrace alternative medicines. In addition to what you would call Board Certified Licensed Physicians, we have acupuncturists, naturopaths, foot reflexologists, even a faith healer. Our sister village New Maya City of Worlds is overrun with chiropractors, but they tend to go more for yoga and body twisting there."

Randall looked thoughtful for a moment. "There is actually one other place to seek medical treatment. We keep a doctor on staff for the tourists at the hotel. We treat a lot of sprains and sunburns and an occasional broken bone, but nothing serious."

The Cardinal raised an issue. "What do you do for death and dying?" he asked.

"We believe in death with dignity," said Ravi. "There are three hospices on site. And before you ask, we accommodate all faiths, Your Eminence. Including Candomble, Umbanda, Zoroastrian, and Christian Coptic."

"The faiths of my continent," muttered Kenji, hearing the words.

"Yes, Kenji," said Randall. "We share more in common than you imagine. There are as many ways to God as there are people, and we embrace all forms of worship."

The door to the tiny hospital opened and they turned to see Van Dorn exit the building. He was smiling, pleasant.

"Good report from the Doctor?" asked the General.

"I feel a little lightheaded," said Van Dorn.

Harmon sneered, a haught of air escaping his nose.

"Like your prescription drugs, Rothschild, our treatments are not without side effects," said Randall. "It should pass soon. Miss Carver, you're next." He held the door open for her. As she entered the building the door closed and Randall turned to continue talking to the tour. "How was your experience with the Doctor, Franklin?" he asked. "You get your problem solved?"

"I had a pain in my chest," said Van Dorn. "He treated it with some kind of curious flashlight that emitted very specific beams of light. I don't know what to make of it."

"Did you take any pills or drugs? Did he give you any injections?" asked the General.

"No. Nothing of the sort," said Van Dorn. "We sorta just talked, very briefly, and he shined a light and said everything should be fine. Just breathe normal. The chest pains will go away in a few days."

"You feel better?" asked Randall.

"Yes," said Van Dorn. "He also said I should stop fretting about my mother's death. Forgive my brothers and my sister. Love them. He said they're all I have left." He looked thoughtful for a moment. "Now, how'd he know about that?"

70

Baba Randall looked off into the distance for a moment. "The doctor tells me he wants to spend more time with Miss Carver. She can catch up with us later. Perhaps we should move on and visit the museum and afterwards the performing arts center. There is a modern dance presentation scheduled that I'd like to see. How about you, Franklin? You up for some dance?"

Van Dorn smiled, a wide grin that made him feel young again. "I haven't danced in years. Sounds like fun."

9

Julie Ann entered the room hesitantly. It was dark and quiet, not what she expected. "Hello?" she asked.

A soft masculine voice came out of the darkness. "Please remove your clothing and stand against the far wall."

It was the last thing she expected. "What?"

"You must be completely naked for me to diagnose you," said the voice.

"Who are you?" she asked nervously

"Enlightened Master Wednesday Djwhal Rampa," came the response.

"Where is the Doctor?" she asked.

"He and I are one in the same," said Rampa. "Now, please remove your clothes and stand next to the dark wall."

This was insane. His requests were not the normal ones made by her doctor. "Maybe I should just skip the naked exam," she said. She turned towards the door searching for the handle in the darkness.

"If you do not remove your clothes, I will never be able to get a good look at the cancer," said the doctor.

It stopped her cold. "How did you know I have cancer?"

"I can see it," said Rampa. "Thriving in your ovaries."

Julie Ann made a sound of acknowledgment. "Uh-huh," she said. "You saw my medical records. I was diagnosed just before this trip. How did you find out so quickly?"

"I found out when I first looked at you," he said. "It's obvious, the discoloration in your midsection, the shooting rays of black, negative energy. If you would remove your clothes, I could take a closer look. It may be curable."

"How do you know these things?" she asked.

"I see it in your aura," he said. "I have the gift of *Sight*."

She hesitated, thinking about it. Curiosity got the best of her. She began to unbutton her blouse. "Yeah, well, okay. You wouldn't be the first man to see me naked," she said.

Her vision had adjusted to the darkness. There was light, but barely enough to tell her surroundings, almost like she sensed things rather than saw them. She slowly removed her clothes, placing them on a chair beside her. She felt self conscious standing in front of a stranger naked. Nevertheless, she moved over to the wall and stood against it.

Master Wednesday Djwhal Rampa stared at her, his eyes out of focus, seeing colors and light instead of darkness. He looked at her ovaries where dark black spots floated in front of her and hid the light of her aura from view. Almost like a virtual reality experience, he reached out with his hands. Colors seemed to emanate from his fingertips as he psychically touched the cancerous growths. Images escaped from the dark spots as he

73

placed his hands over each of them. He saw her angry husband, a stillborn fetus, her crying on the floor behind a closed bedroom door. He sighed, breathing deeply, then opened his mind and drank it all in, an impression that told the whole story in a glance.

"Left ovary, I see the pain," he said. "What did your regular doctor recommend?"

"Surgery," she said. "Followed by chemotherapy. I wasn't sure if I would do it."

"Why?" he asked.

She winced, the memories returning to her like forgotten children in a nursing home. "I watched my mother go through chemo when she had her cancer. I knew I was prone. I told myself I wasn't going to die like her, a weak creature drained by the cure as much as the disease."

"I see," he said. "I can remove it if you like. Some diseases are karmic. Yours is not. Merely the result of some negative energy that unfortunately settled in your uterus. I see you carry the guilt of a failed relationship. You lost the child, and along with it the man."

"How'd you know that?" she asked. "You do have my medical records."

"I see it in your past," he said. "Stored as memories in the DNA. Your uterus wanted that child to live, but your husband did not."

"He told me he didn't want children," she said.

"All men say that at first," he said. "They react in fear to the responsibility."

She continued living the past. "I told him I was pregnant. I could feel his anger after that. Storming around the house like an old

74

bear, swiping at me like I was some kind of open honey jar."

"And you accepted his anger," he said. "It settled in the uterus, a negative energy that fed off the fetus until there was nothing left. The child never stood a chance."

She began to cry, the memories too strong to hold back the sea of tears. "Not long after that my water broke in the middle of the night. I woke him up. He grumbled and went back to sleep. Told me where to find the car keys. Said he'd drive me to the hospital in the morning if I was still there. I went back to sleep, a towel wadded up between my legs. The next morning I felt really sick to my stomach, pains in my abdomen. He took me to the doctor but it was already obvious to me. I found a tiny stillborn fetus in the towel. I cried all the way to the hospital. He thought I was in pain, and I guess I was, just emotional pain and not so much physical."

"It's good to cry," said the Master. "Breaks down old programming."

She composed herself and continued. "I left him soon after that, but the pain never went away. And now I have cancer." The tears began to flow like broken plumbing.

"It is treatable," said the Master. "You know the cause, you have just described it to me. It is time to let go. If you are ready to do that, it can be removed."

It was the most hopeful thing she had heard since the diagnosis. Finally, a doctor who understood her pain. "Really? Then you think I should have the surgery?"

The Master smiled. "If you wish, but I can remove it right now if you're ready."

She looked hopeful. "You have an operating room? How much will it cost me? What kind of insurance do you accept?"

75

The Master laughed. "Come, lie down over here," he said. He touched a hidden button and the lights came up slowly to reveal the room. There was a massage table off to the side. He gently pat the table indicating where she should go.

"Should I put my clothes back on?" she asked.

"Not necessary," he said.

She moved toward the table, covering herself with her hands.

"No need for false modesty here," he said. "I am a professional."

"Good," she said. "I'd hate to sue you for sexual harassment."

The Master laughed.

"What's so funny?" she asked.

"I am celibate," he said. "As a man I mastered sexuality long ago. Used it to raise my consciousness, not feed my desires. I had a wife, sired children. Nothing advanced my spiritual growth more than having a family. The dynamics of close, interpersonal relationships force us to make choices. We serve each other in love."

She slowly sat down on the table, her hands still hiding her treasures. He looked into her eyes and all shame seemed to disappear. She dropped her hands to her sides. "What happened to them? Your family, I mean?"

"They grew up," he said. "My children are all married, my wife has moved on."

"You're divorced?' she asked.

"We still see each other," he said. "For much of our life we worked together, raised a family, then we just developed different interests after that. The children were gone, and the desire for sex faded as well. It didn't make sense to intrude on each other's space. We are much happier apart."

He slowly lowered her onto the table until she laid gently on her back. He took out a bowl of water and a chicken egg, lit a candle and held out a plate in front of Julie Ann.

"Do you have an offering?" he asked.

"Offering?"

"It can be anything," he said. "Money, a trinket, something personal."

She sneered. "There's always a cost, isn't there?"

"No cost," he said. "Only an offering."

"Get my purse," she said. "I have just the thing."

He obliged. She removed a small necklace from it and held it out for inspection. "This was my mother's. It's not worth much, it's just costume jewelry. But it meant a lot to her. And to me, I guess."

"Perfect," he said. "Set it on the tray."

She complied and he took the tray and placed it in front of a statue of Jesus on a alter in the corner of the room. She could see other offerings, trinkets, pictures of people, scribbles on shreds of paper.

"Now relax," he said, turning towards her. "Breathe deep."

She closed her eyes following his request, drawing air into her lungs as he suggested.

77

"Deeper," he said. "Expand the lungs until they can hold no more. Just a few deep breaths. Let the life giving prana flow into you."

She obeyed.

"Now, try to relax. I'm not going to hurt you. There will be no pain, just a slight pressure."

The Master began to chant. He raised his hands several times, touched her gently, reassuringly. He placed the egg on her navel, continuing to pray and chant.

She looked around nervously. Candles burned, she thought she heard primitive drums in the background. The Master's arms raised in blind ceremony and the room began to spin. He mumbled unintelligible words, a chorus of voices joining him from the unknown. The drums grew louder, the room spun about her. She felt dizzy, a strong desire to get up and leave.

Suddenly it all stopped and there was silence in the room. The Master gently removed the egg from her stomach and broke it over the bowl of water. A dark, inky semi-liquid poured out of the egg, thick, viscous, and ugly. The Master looked deep into it, then at her abdomen.

"You're in luck," he said. "I think I got it all. You can put your clothes back on." He went to a nearby sink, disposed of the egg and water bowl, and washed his hands.

She sat upright on the table. "That was weird," she said.

The Master returned to her side. "How do you feel?"

She rubbed her stomach and smiled. "Like I can bend in the middle. There aren't any rocks in my stomach anymore."

The Master gently placed his hand on her abdomen. "Yes. We got it all!"

She laughed nervously. "Thank you. That's it, then?"

"That's it," he said.

"Should I see my doctor when I get back home?"

"If you wish," he said. "But it's not necessary."

"Say, where'd you get your degree?" she asked. "What kind of doctor are you? Oncologist?"

"A curandero," he said.

"What?"

"A curandero," he repeated. "Medicine man."

She still didn't get it. He made funny eyes at her as he said, "A witch doctor."

10

Kenji stood in the bathroom in front of the urinal wishing he was using his penis for more exciting things than peeing. Thoughts of Nan filled his mind. Something about her fascinated him. His thoughts were interrupted as Sun Ki Han walked into the room and stood at the urinal beside him. He turned to look at him. "At least their toilets are the same," he said to Han. "Can't say that I expected anything different."

"These Roman toilets are for the tourists," said Sun. "They crap and piss in little buckets and use humanure in the fields."

"I know." said Alamoto "I don't know whether to call their agriculture primitive or advanced. It's a puzzle."

Sun turned to face the man. "Something I wanted to talk to you about, Alamoto."

Kenji's eyes narrowed. He has expected trouble from Han. "I had a feeling there was a reason you followed me into the bathroom."

Sun stood defiantly, looked Kenji in the eye. "I've been watching you put the moves on my wife all afternoon."

"EX-wife," corrected Kenji.

"Yeah. Whatever," said Sun. "I'm telling you. I don't like what I see."

"And what is it you see?"

"You!" said Sun. "Getting in the way of my relationship. You know I agreed to come on this mission just to see her and patch things up."

"It doesn't appear that she wants that," said Kenji. "She speaks of you with disdain and hatred."

"You're lying," said Sun. "Nan is incapable of hatred."

"Maybe so," said Kenji. "But it's her love I'm interested in, not her hatred."

"I'm telling you to leave her alone," said Sun.

Kenji packed his equipment back in his trousers and moved in close to Sun, speaking in a low, threatening voice. "Listen, you little peacock. You have no right telling me who I can and cannot flirt with." His eyes narrowed, his nostrils flared. "Listen carefully. I'm only going to tell you this once. If you ever say anything like this to me again, I will rip that tiny penis of yours out from between your legs and shove it down your miserable throat. Now get out of my way. I'm anxious to get back to the tour."

Sun stepped aside, showing no sign of fear. Alamoto casually walked over to the sink and washed his hands, his eyes studying his adversary intently in the mirror. Sun zipped his pants up, passed on washing his hands and quickly left the room. Outside Nan was waiting for Kenji. Sun stopped, staring at her, saying nothing. She stared back, hard as diamonds. Kenji finally emerged from the restroom. She smiled and offered him her arm which he graciously accepted. They gently walked away, the sound of laughter and intimate conversation filling the hallway.

"Did I tell you what a bright soul you are, Kenji," said Nan, loud enough for Sun to hear. "I expected an African warlord, but you're something different. A leader. A spiritual God-king to your people."

Sun watched them for a moment, shook his head and skulked away.

11

At first there was the void of space, what God would call the Firmament. It is also written into our history that God said, "Let there be Light," and so there was. But God also created Darkness at the same moment, a contrast and anchor to help the Light shine brighter.

Dark and Light forces played with each other as the Hand of God formed creation. They came together, swirling like yin-yang, catching each other's eye, attracting each other as opposites do. There was a hint of sexual interplay on a scale so grand we can hardly imagine it. By the creative will of God and the energy given to them, they joined, giving birth to what would become our Mother Earth.

Like all newborns, the planet cried, a spattering of volcanic and seismic activity, a turbulent world where light and dark could meet. She began to spin, dancing to the rhythm of the cosmos. Nurtured by the energy of the sun, she slowly matured, turning green and blue over time.

And they named their child Gaia, a complex world born of both light and dark. Like all living things, and do not deceive yourself, a planet is living, she aspired to a destiny of her own. Like everything in the Universe, she has a soul that carries the spark of the Creator. Like everything in the Universe, she knew that her lifetime was finite, that one day she would ascend to a higher level and be reunited with the source of all life. Yes, the Divine Plan is in effect, even in this part of the Universe.

Gaia agreed to host life and the Creator brought forth a multitude of plants and animals combining the Spark of Life with the matter and elements of the Earth. God looked upon this and said it was good. Then one day a new species took root, one called Man, another creation born of Divine Source, and God said this was good. But Gaia did not agree. As the new species grew and flourished, Gaia grew sick. Rather than forming a partnership with Gaia, Man in his arrogance claimed dominance of the planet and did not recognize her divine spirit. The beautiful, blue green planet gradually grew darker during the day from poisons and pollution, brighter at night from electricity and too many lights.

Many atrocities were committed, some inadvertently, some intentionally. Oil spills, chemical releases, air pollution, open pit mines, scars on the Earth. Names were given to some. Agent Orange, Napalm, Love Canal, Gulf Horizon, Exxon-Valdez. Man slowly sucked the life out of the planet until one day Gaia shuttered, no longer able to fight the illness, she began to think that she had come to the end of her days.

What to do about Man?

Rothschild got up from his seat, pushed his way to the aisle and headed for the exit. "I've had enough of this rubbish," he said. "As far as museum films go, I give this one a two."

A few of the others got up and followed him as if he were the next item on today's tour. Juliana and the General stayed, as did Van Dorn. "This is interesting," he said, focusing back on the film.

Outside, the conversation continued. "It's a dramatization," said Barclay.

"It's an effrontery," said Rothschild. "The only part that you got right was that God created Man. That much is true. But now I

84

know for sure you people don't read the Bible because it says right in Genesis that God gave man dominion of the planet and all the animals that He created for us."

"Really?" said the Cardinal "I thought that *dominion* was only one translation. Some say it reads that God gave us *stewardship* over the Earth. Still another source says God made us *responsible* for the Earth."

"Not in my version of the Bible," said Chase. "I'm no Catholic. And neither is Harmon."

"Gentlemen, let's not start a debate over versions of the Bible."

"Why not?" asked Barclay. "As long as we recognize that it is not really the Bible we are debating, but our individual beliefs."

"Ah," said Randall. "A much better topic. I have a theory. I suggest that a thinking man first chooses what to believe, then finds the supporting material. A weaker man is told what to believe, and does not question it."

"I think people miss the intent of the Bible when they focus too hard on the wording," said Singh. "Zealots are sometimes like lawyers defending the letter of the law and not the purpose. Nobody likes their beliefs challenged. We all like to stay in our comfort zone."

"It's all there," said the Cardinal. "Jesus spoke in parables to keep things simple. It's man that makes it complicated."

"Well spoken, Jameson," said Randall. "Look, I may believe the Bible to be a flawed work, just like anything handed down from antiquity. Humanity itself is a flawed work."

"The Bible is not flawed!" shouted Rothschild.

"The Bible is half truth, half lies, and the rest fables."

"Gentlemen, gentlemen, please," said the Cardinal. "Let's focus on the meaning. Peace on Earth. Love your brothers and sisters. Surely this is the message of the Bible. But if you wish, perhaps at the next meeting of the Ecumenical Council I will suggest that we rephrase the old courtroom speech. Say, put your hand on the Bible and promise to tell the half truth, the half lies, and nothing but the fables so help me God."

Barclay and Singh started to laugh. Chase joined in and soon so did Randall and Morgan.

"Ah, Cardinal Jameson. For a Holy Man, you have quite a sense of humor," said Randall.

"So do you, Baba Randall," said Jameson.

The tour moved on.

12

They had become a disorganized bunch, but tour was trying to assemble again, members of the groups coming together from different venues. Impatient, some went out exploring and scouting on their own. Singh and the Cardinal stood together near a designated meeting place talking while they waited for the others. They leaned against a railing watching a group of flamingos bathe in a lake. Most of the birds stood in the shallow water nudging the underside of their wings with their bright beaks. The crystal mountain towered in the distance standing out from its neighbors. Cardinal Jameson stared at it, his eyes tracing the path of the tram as he followed a train coming down from the other side of the mountain.

"I don't know why everyone wouldn't want to live here," he said.

"I would like to think that we could remake the world into this rather than move everyone here," said Singh.

"I enjoyed this morning's tour," said Jameson. "I must admit, your hospice facilities are beyond anything I have ever seen. So much effort into the act of dying."

"Death is a spiritual process," said Singh. "It's necessary. There is so much unnecessary fear about dying, but not here in the Village."

"God puts that fear in us to stay alive," said the Cardinal.

"Maybe so," said Singh. "But if people knew the truth, they would fear birth."

"Why do you say that?"

"When we die, we lose our physical body and we are left with our spirit form," said Singh. "People on the Earth plane can feel your presence, and you can read their thoughts. They grieve, for only through death do we realize the depth of our love for those who have passed. But more importantly, when we die we are surrounded by loved ones, we are one with God again and the cloud of earthly illusion is lifted. We confront our own truth and we become our Oversoul. In birth, we are taken from this environment, shoved into a tiny, helpless body that takes years to master before we can even begin to communicate and bond with the loved ones around us. We forget everything, our multi dimensional memory wiped clean as part of this process. We are separated from Divine Source, making it necessary to find and forge that relationship again. No, Your Grace, if people knew the truth, they would fear birth, not death."

"I tend to agree with you," said the Cardinal. "If we knew how beautiful Heaven was, we'd all want to die and end this life of suffering."

"Why does it have to be a life of suffering?" asked Singh. "Look at what we've done here."

"It's remarkable, but very unconventional," said the Cardinal.

"Just the opposite," said Singh. "It's a model for humanity to build on. This is how things can be. Let the outside world look at us and say, *Hey! It can work. We can all thrive.*"

Jameson sighed. "I agree with you there, Singh. I'm tired of politics, even within the Church. I see great men struggle with ambition, lust, greed, all manner of sin. Priests lead busy lives, at least the good ones do. The mediocre ones, they sit in the rectory, meet their obligatory schedule, and worry about their creature comforts. They age and soon forget why they became men of the cloth."

"Speaking of priestly duties, thank you for administering last rights to that old lady, Cardinal. It was nice of you to oblige her."

The Cardinal nodded. "I didn't think I would find devout Catholics here."

"We embrace all faiths," said Singh.

"I see that now," said Jameson. "It does my soul good to see so many faiths coexist. I never understood why Christian must fight Muslim who fights Jew. It saddens me that Christians even fight Christians."

"Do you think that there is one true faith, Cardinal?" asked Singh.

"I've been taught that, and I've also been taught to be tolerant," said Jameson.

Singh nodded in agreement. "A wise teacher, you had."

The Cardinal looked around, took in the scenery and breathed deep. "I don't know what it is, Singh. Maybe it's the fresh air, the food, the company, of course. But I'm beginning to feel good. Like I used to when I first became a priest. God, I was so idealistic."

"So was I," said Singh. He stopped and turned to the Cardinal seeing the perplexed look on his face. "I spent several lifetimes in the priesthood, two of them Catholic," he explained.

Jameson laughed and gave Singh a slight nod of his head. "I don't think I'll ever get used to you talking like that. I forget you remember past lives. You see, I believe we have one life, one chance to serve the Lord."

Singh nodded back. "In my native country everybody believes in reincarnation. It makes them lazy sometimes. They get complacent or don't want to work so hard. Say things like, *Oh, if I don't complete my task this lifetime, I'll just come back and do it again.* Some people also have a lot of trouble dealing with their Karma when they find out they were a princess last time and they have to be a waitress or a scullery maid this time. I believe this is the reason we are wiped clean at the beginning of each lifetime. I've sometimes watched a superior attitude develop as one life bleeds into the next."

"So, what's it like for you, remembering all that stuff, all your past accomplishments, your past lifetimes?" asked the Cardinal.

"It's very reassuring," said Singh. "And it adds to my experience here immensely. My past lives are very compartmentalized, and I access them much as I would a library of video clips. I replay what I want to watch and put it away when I'm done. And through this process I see how all my lives have all led to this moment of focus. I can even see what's in store for me next. How about you, Cardinal. What's in store for you next?"

Jameson again took in the beauty of the Village, the natural surroundings, the animals, the people. "I'm not sure, Singh," he said.

"You could come here and work," said Cameron. "Be our Vatican representative. Help humanity the way you wanted to when you were a young priest." He thought he saw a tear in the Cardinal's eye.

"What you offer is great, my son," said Jameson. "I forget sometimes that Christ lives in my heart. You know, I think I would like what you propose. The more I see of your Village, the more I like. But I could use one more thing to convince me. Can you do me a favor?"

"What's that, Your Grace?" asked Singh.

"You have a Catholic Church here, you say?"

"Yes."

"Good," said the Cardinal. "Could you take me there? I want to skip the rest of the tour. I have an urge to conduct the evening service. It's been a long time since I've said Mass."

Singh smiled and the two walked off as the General and Juliana arrived. They saw Singh and the Cardinal walking away, but they didn't care. They were lost in their own world. Juliana had a glow about her, a high priestess with a powerful aura. The General warmed himself in her glow. They enjoyed light conversation, moving through her world gently. He felt the beginnings of a budding relationship, something, being a single man, that he had not felt in a long time.

"Why, General," she said continuing their talk. "I didn't realize you were such a culinary expert."

"I love the vegetables you have here," he said. "Lunch was excellent. I grew up on a farm, used to fresh food until I left home. I learned to cook out of necessity. You'll have to try my veal tenderloins sometime."

Juliana frowned. "Sorry. I don't eat meat."

"Oh. I forgot," said the General.

"You know, taste is really an underrated sense," she said.

"I feel the same way," said Whiteweather. "All my life I've been looking for that bite of food that sends me to heaven."

"Really?" said Juliana. "Every cook in the world is looking for that." She smiled. "I think I have just the thing for you, love. Let's ditch this tour and head to a nearby cafe for an afternoon treat."

Whiteweather smiled back. "Well, I just can't say no to a proposition like that from a pretty lady."

"Let's go, then. I'll take you on a personal tour of the village and show you whatever you want."

"I'd enjoy that," said Whiteweather.

"Tell me, General," she said. "What other senses do you enjoy? How do you feel about Touch, for instance?" She rubbed up against him, tousling his hair and watching him smile like a fourteen year old farm boy. They walked off together, merging into the beauty of the city. Animals and birds turned their heads watching the buds of romance grow between them, for what creature does not enjoy seeing a couple in love? As they strolled away, Juliana reared her head back and laughed out loud. The General gently reached over and wrapped his hand in hers. They walked off unnoticed just as Baba Randall, Chase, and Rothschild arrived.

"So, you don't believe in a free education system?" asked Randall.

"The whole purpose of our education system is to teach the lower classes to stand in line and respect authority," said Rothschild. "That's why it takes twelve years."

"Yeah," said Chase. "That's why we made the Great Depression in the nineteen thirties. To break the spirit of the American man, take away his dignity, his land, home and family, and make him stand in line for soup and crackers for ten years. Then we took all the gold and silver and left them holding nothing but monopoly money. That's why the Americans are a defeated population."

Rothschild glared. "You just don't know when to shut up and be quiet, do you, Chase."

The conversation stagnated for a moment before Randall said, "As far as education goes, I disagree with you Harmon. Look at our system here in the Village. We have seventeen year olds that have achieved a PHD. They love their subject matter so much that they study full time, no summer vacations. Amazing what people will do when they find their passion."

"What you just described is an anomaly," said Rothschild. "Teenagers are only passionate about dating, driving cars, and getting away from their parents."

"That's all I wanted to do," said Chase. "My Dad *made* me go to college."

"Where you did exactly the same thing," said Rothschild.

Chase looked down at the ground chastened once again. Randall rebooted the conversation. "One thing missing in public school is spiritual education," he said.

"That's why we have private school," said Rothschild.

Randall pointed out what he saw as a flaw. "So only a small population is exposed to religious teachings?"

"Those that need spiritual education go to Sunday school at their church," said Rothschild. "Religious education is the responsibility of the parents, not the State."

"I see," said Randall. "So you allow sex education in the schools but not religious teaching?"

"The parents protest anything to do with religion," said Rothschild.

"Prayer in the schools was abolished long ago."

"Only because you chose a narrow approach to it," said Randall. "It's important to our humanity to understand all religions, not just the faith of our fathers."

"Let's get off this merry go round, Randall," said Rothschild. "Just admit we have different views and move on."

"If you wish. How about we go to evening meditation?"

Rothschild laughed. "How about instead we go have a drink?"

"I don't consume alcohol," said Randall.

Rothschild sneered. "Another point we differ on."

A short distance away, Barclay was talking to Van Dorn while they waited.

"I wish I knew what that doctor did to me," said Van Dorn. "I haven't felt this high since my college days."

"You say he shined a light in your eye?" asked Barclay.

"And used a crystal," said Van Dorn.

"You ever heard of aromatherapy?" asked Barclay.

"Of course," said Van Dorn. "Inhaling something that induces peace and tranquility. They make candles and such for it. Of course, there are some smells that make me gag, although I wouldn't class them as therapy."

"Just as smells can induce a certain response, so can light," said Barclay. "We have found through our research that colors have effects on the human body as well. By matching the color to a

94

person's aura we can create a kind of resonance, not only doubling someone's ability, but also inducing a state of higher consciousness."

Van Dorn was curious. "Now why would the doctor do that to treat chest pains?"

"To cure a disease you sometimes need to get to the root of it," said McKenner.

"That still doesn't explain why I feel all light and happy," said Van Dorn.

"Because you've been cured!" said Barclay. "What you're experiencing is the feeling of being healthy and alive."

"It's good to be alive," remarked Van Dorn.

"You said it," said Barclay. "You know what makes me feel alive? A swim in the ocean. How about an afternoon swim?"

"I've been wanting to do that since ever since I got here," said Van Dorn.

"What are we waiting for?" said Barclay. "Let's go."

13

The restaurant Juliana took him to was unlike anything the General expected. The outside looked modest, no garish lighting or advertised menu. A small placard fixed beside a set of red double doors announced in block letters that they had arrived at the Bhakti Kitchen. On the door to the right a sign hung on a string from a nail, hand scripted in ornate calligraphy, *Welcome. We Are Open.* He started to head for it but she gently took him by the hand and led him behind the restaurant and straight into the kitchen.

It was not a conventional restaurant kitchen. In his estimate it took up half the building. Nobody was cramped for space and the areas were divided up by task. At a large wooden table, a cook garnished vegetables with spices. The spices came from live plants located in a greenhouse that bordered the kitchen and the dining area. A chef sipped from a cauldron filled with soup suspended over a large open pit fire. Skewers of vegetable kabobs roasted gently near the soup. In a different area a woman took warm bread out of a clay oven while another gently sliced fresh loaves and put the pieces in baskets. There was a prep chef praying over a salad while another gently chopped vegetables, no hurry, mindfully focused on his task. He looked up at the General and said, "Chopping vegetables is love."

From behind him, the head chef Aaron gently placed his hand on the man's shoulder. "Yes, it is Shanti. Yes it is. Love is the main ingredient we serve around here," he said. "Hello Juliana." He wiped his hands on the side of his apron and reached out to her.

She hugged him and he patted her back gently, sighs of love escaping from deep in his throat. She whispered a few words of peace in his ear before drawing back to introduce her guest. "Chef Aaron, this is General Carson Whiteweather."

Aaron smiled, a man obviously happy in everything he did.

Whiteweather extended his hand. "Call me Carson," he said.

"I prefer a good hug," said Aaron, his arms out, ready to wrap the General in love.

It was hard to resist. Carson smiled. "When in Rome..." he said, his arms placed and ready. As they met he felt something, a movement in his heart, as if he were greeting a long lost brother for the first time.

It felt good.

"Glad to meet you finally," said Aaron his hands clapping the General's back one last time before releasing him. "I heard about you from our public meetings. I looked up your history on the internet. You're quite a man, Carson. You fought a lot of wars and led your country to victory many times."

Whiteweather scowled. "Wars I never started. Finishing other people's business. Sometimes I feel used by the politicians, a lackey in their employ. I may not make the decisions but I have to live with them."

Aaron nodded. "Still, from what I read, your men were lucky to have you in charge. Casualties under your command were at all time lows. You seem to care more about your people than winning a battle."

"Actually I care about both," he said.

"Yes," agreed Aaron "But your strategies must have been well thought through. You compassionately took people into consideration."

Juliana interrupted. "The General is an intelligent and compassionate man," she said. She bumped up against him in a girlish way. "Save the military talk for later, gentlemen. I'm here for one reason. I was telling the General about your quest for the ultimate bite of food."

Aaron's eyes lit up. "Ah! The Nirvana Pie. Yes. One bite and you ascend into higher consciousness."

"It's a myth, my friend," said the General.

"Right, you are," said Aaron. "Elusive." He rubbed his hands together. "But I've come close. At least I think I have. Care to try?"

She bumped up against Carson again and he looked at her and smiled, his eyes alight with glee "I'm game if you are," he said.

Aaron led them through the kitchen and into a large cooler. He retrieved a special container, a futuristic cake keeper, a translucent dome shaped thing that looked like a small water purification plant. A series of tanks, tiny pipes, and valves were attached to the side of the thing. They followed him from there and up a staircase to his office. A small table sat to one side, a humble dining area in his private retreat. He set the dish on the table, pressing the top of the dome. There was a hiss as air sucked into the keeper, a sigh of freshness. Inside was a glowing pie. Whiteweather looked up to see if it was a trick of the lighting, but the pie actually appeared to glow. Aaron carefully carved a slice and placed it on a plate decorated with a pastry doily. He casually invited the General to take a seat, bringing him a clean fork and a napkin.

"The Nirvana Pie," he said. "Let me warn you, one bite will raise

your consciousness. You may not be ready for this."
Whiteweather let out a polite humph. "Chef Aaron, I've eaten in the best restaurants around the world, not to mention my mother's own cooking, bless her soul. I will judge this bite with a critical eye."

Aaron nodded as Whiteweather took a seat and picked up the fork. He took a bite. He chewed twice, then stopped, chewed gently, slow mastication. He smiled, his posture improving as his shoulders braced back. He took a second bite.

He felt a bright white light around him, a warmth in his stomach that spread to his heart and finally to every corner of his body. He shut his eyes and when he opened them it was a vision from his past.

He was in a farm house, the one he grew up in, sitting like he had so many times as a boy at the wooden dinner table his grandfather had made. He heard humming and turned to see his Mother over by the stove. She turned and offered him a plate of food. He took it. It was the Nirvana Pie.

"Nothing like down home cooking to make ya' feel good," she said.

"Thanks. Mom," was all he could say.

He noticed two bites were missing, much of the pie remaining. The fork was in his hand. He carved out a piece and took another bite. He closed his eyes, the taste doing it to him again, as if he didn't already feel good enough. He tingled, closing his eyes. Angels appeared around him in the darkness. When he opened his eyes, they were still there. He stood up from the table, looking out the window. It was heaven, the sun setting, clouds parting to light the sky with bright yellow rays. The General's face illuminated as he turned towards the Light.

He whispered softy, tears of joy coming to his eyes. "Look Juliana. I see God."

His mother answered him but it was her voice. "Yes, you do. Now, go to Him. Follow your bliss. Open your heart."

He looked down at the pie on the table. It exploded into tiny pieces of white light fading like fireworks to become a part of fabric of everything in the room. Outside he could see the same light calling to him, beginning to warm his face with heat unlike any he had ever felt.

He stood up from the table and moved towards the window. A sudden darkness passed over his heart, a dark haze of smoke. The view of heaven became blocked, distant and apart from what was happening in the foreground. He saw a battle raging, explosions, men falling in combat, blood on the ground, dirt and grime on every face.

The angels tried to move him on, but he loitered. "I know this battle," he said. "Many people died on my orders here. I brought so much death into the world."

He heard an angel whisper in his ear. "Other men brought the violence. You made death your puppet, dancing on the stage of life where his scythe would do the least damage."

"Many people lived because of you, Carson," he heard his mother say, but again it was Juliana's voice. "It's time to forgive yourself. You can't change the past, only your future."

Carson fought the ultimate battle, not outward but against himself. "I lost many men in this battle. Bad choices. I was so young. It may have turned the tide of war but at what cost?" Demons seemed to agree with him. He looked down, one withered hand held his while the other pointed away from the Light. The General squinted, the fog of war moving across his face. He smelled cordite and sulfur, napalm and rotting flesh. The light in the distance he now saw was a fire burning bright and hot as a magnesium flare.

"Time to go," said the demon.

The General went to move but he was blocked. He looked down, realized he was standing in front of the old Dutch door that led out of the kitchen. He had been staring out through the open top half of the door. The demon gently reached down and opened the bottom half. "This way please. Let me guide you."

The General stepped outside. The demon closed the door, no turning back. There were tears born of pain in Carson's eyes. His heart was laden with guilt, sins that would not let him walk free. Before he could take another step, a young Lieutenant appeared in front of him.

"I'm here to report. All is well, sir."

"What's that?" asked Carson.

The demon tugged at his wrist impatiently.

A rough old Sargent materialized beside the Lieutenant speaking over his shoulder. "Come on, General," he said. "There's nothing over there but a ruined battlefield."

"Yes, Sir," said the Lieutenant. "General Hanson sent me personally to escort you."

"Hanson?" said the General. "Bucky Hanson? I thought he was dead."

The demon tugged at his wrist again. Carson looked down at the withered hand, then back up into the piercing blue eyes of the Lieutenant.

"Bucky Hanson?" said the General. "Sure would like to see him again."

"Come on, General. We've moved on. Come with us. We'll show you the way to the front."

He looked beside him and the demon was gone, an angel in its place. The withered hand was now an open palm that shimmered and invited him to take it. He looked up, the table, his mother and the farm fading into a bright light. Music gently filled the air as the dark fog cleared and gleaming lights shone in the distance. A crowd of people beckoned to him, beings so bright he could not see their faces.

The Lieutenant shouldered his rifle, and that was when the General noticed it wasn't a rifle at all but rather a golden staff that sang of times gone by. It lit the way in a new direction as they slowly walked into the light.

"All has been forgiven," whispered the angel. "All that remains is for you to forgive yourself."

The tears flowed out of his eyes now, no longer emissaries of pain. He felt forgiveness in his heart, not only for himself, but for the superiors who gave him tough orders to follow, for the people who had wronged him in the past, for the driver who had irritated him on the freeway last week, for the farmhands who had teased him and played pranks on when he was a kid, for Susan, the woman who had hurt him in ways he did not think possible.

It grew until he felt forgiveness for all humanity. He felt it as he voiced the words.

"Forgive them Father, for they know not what they do."

14

The evening had been more perfect than any he could remember. Kenji Alamoto had eaten the best meal ever, seen a performance that left him breathless, and now he was alone with the company of a beautiful and intelligent woman. The contours of her shape moved and inspired him like poetry, but it was the conversation that captured his heart. She caught him staring more than once at her feminine charms, his eyes quickly darting away like a schoolboy caught sneaking a glance at a dirty picture.

He waved the card key to his hotel room in front of the security lock. It clicked gently, admitting him to his private suite. "Won't you come in for a minute?" he asked.

Nan didn't hesitate. "I was hoping you would ask," she said.

He opened the door and they walked in. Lights came on automatically, the room making itself hospitable. The scent of natural flowers hung in the air, vases in the room filled with them. He closed the door gently behind her.

Outside, Sun peered from around the corner at the end of the corridor. *She went in the room*, he thought. His teeth gritted, his fists balled. He stared at the shut door until the elevator made a ding down at the end of the corridor. It jarred him enough to move away, down the hall and up the stairs to his own room.

Once there, he went to the bed and reached deep under the mattress retrieving a ceremonial knife he had smuggled into the community. He held it up, stared at it, twisted it, light reflecting, glinting off the polished surface, a look of madness in his eye. He tucked it under his belt and started to leave.

On the way out he passed a mirror. He saw himself, stopped, and looked deeply. A shadow passed over his face. His eyes seemed tired, his skin saggy. His pallor was pasty and his face etched with worry lines. He looked down at his hand. It was trembling. He tried to make it stop, looking at it like an unruly child. He finally balled his hand into a fist and beat it against his side. He looked up and into his eyes staring blankly at his reflection, his thoughts lost in the emptiness. Finally he turned abruptly and left the room.

15

Kenji laid face down on the bed, his shirt off, Nan gently rubbing his back. "You have a lot of deep seated tension. Lesions lying beneath the surface."

"I shoulder the responsibility of my people," said Kenji.

"All great leaders carry the burden. Let me help."

He turned over, touching her gently, smiling, enthralled with her. His mind raced to distant mountains he would scale with her, peaks in life he had never experienced. Oh, yes. There had been women in his past, but none like this. Her eyes were deep, sparkling with a dynamic energy he could not define. When she looked at him, he felt like he was in a bubble alone with her, a soapy film of iridescence coloring their world bright and hopeful.

And now she wanted to help him. He reached out and gently took her hand, the one that had been rubbing him so soft yet firm. Somehow she had taken away years of set-in tension and constant pain, the war wounds and the legacy of his climb to power. He stroked her hand gently and then lifted it to his lips. The kiss was deep, full of emotion, and stronger than any he would have given her lips.

Nan sighed, a deep breath of air clearing and energizing her all at once.

"And what can you do?" he asked, thinking of a thousand ways she could help him.

She looked down at his crotch, the conspicuous bulge in his pants. "Well, for one thing, I can take care of that," she said. "You must like me. I see the excitement in your eyes, the sexual energy building."

"I could take you now. Make you appreciate a good man," he said.

She put her hand to his cheek and drew closer. "I already appreciate you, Kenji," she said.

"Then what are you waiting for?" he asked.

Nan pulled back, locked her hands behind her back and stretched like a cat. "I'm letting my energy and my excitement build," she said. "I am a Tantric Goddess, Ken. I can help you channel that forceful energy properly. I practice and strengthen certain pelvic muscles that make sex with me extra pleasurable."

He started to unbutton his pants but she stopped him, petting him gently. "Not so fast, tiger," she said. "Let me explain something. Rather than come in me, full of carnal lust, we will join together, one *Being* fulfilled and free of all desire."

Kenji was anxious. "Yes. Yes. I want that. To join with you."

She began to talk slowly, her words seeping out like intellectual foreplay. She reached down and touched the underside of his penis, drawing her fingers around to gently grasp his erection. "When you orgasm, I will use my muscles to redirect that energy back into you," she said. "You will feel a connection between your base down here, the root chakra where your penis is, and the crown chakra, your brain, the gateway to higher consciousness." She let go of his penis, her hand moving up the back of his spine, tracing the sacred channels up and into his crown chakra where she

106

tousled his hair and created a small energy vortex above his head.

He could feel it. Sexual behavior for him, for most men, is just the opposite. Sex starts in the brain and works its way down into the penis. Fantasies and wishes, combined with events in the past that shaped these fantasies, create the need for sex in a man's mind. Impulses can be resisted. An undisciplined man falls into warped ideas of how to deal with his sexual energy. He easily becomes a creature of habit as unchecked and misdirected fantasies bloom into nightmares. But what she proposed was the opposite of anything he had considered.

"You will have an orgasm unlike anything you've experienced before," she said.

"Is that so?"

"That's okay, as long as the energy takes a round trip," she said. "I want some of it too." She rubbed up against him, slowly running her fingers up and down his back. His breath quickened. Nan slowly took off her shirt, rubbed her hands across Kenji's chest muscles, drawing in close for the kiss.

There was a knock at the door. They stopped breathing.

The knock came again.

Kenji looked at her, then at the door. "Go away," he said.

From the other side of the door came a voice, deep and authoritative. "Peace Officer Kransky. Village security. Please open up."

They quickly got up, put their shirts back on. The bed was a mess as they stood up, thrown back covers, crushed pillows, and rumpled sheets. Kenji answered the door. Officer Kransky stood there, tall as they looked up into his eyes. He was holding a sheepish looking Sun by the arm. Sun noticed the rumpled sheets and his eyes momentarily flared. Kransky sensed something and turned to look at him, gripping his arm tighter. Sun calmed himself and the Peace Officer turned to Kenji. "Do you know this man?" he asked.

"Yes," answered Kenji.

Nan pushed her way from behind him. "He's my ex-husband," she said, turning towards Sun. "What is it?" she asked him. "What do you want?"

He didn't answer. Kransky hesitated, then filled the void. "He was loitering out here," he said. "Very suspicious behavior. Our psychic down at the station picked up on the negative energy. Sent me here to investigate. I detected second level fight or flee emanations from the back side of his root chakra. Then I notice, not only is he insecure, he has black spots in his heart chakra. Just look at them."

Kenji looked up and down Sun but saw nothing, no black spots on his pants, none on his shirt. Nan, on the other hand, became alarmed. "Why didn't I see this before?"

"He also had this," said Kransky. He opened a pouch at his side and removed the ceremonial knife.

Nan's eyes widened, then squinted, looking hard at her ex-husband. "What were you up to, Sun?"

He hesitated, felt a tight squeeze on his arm from the tall man. "I just wanted to see you. Talk to you," he said.

"With a knife?" said Nan.

He looked down at the floor.

"What should we do with him, Ma'am?" asked Kransky.

"What do you normally do in these cases?" she asked.

"Take him down to the station where we purge the negative energy out of him."

"Sounds like a good thing to do," she said. "Thank you Officer. You may proceed."

"Have a nice evening, ma'am," said Kransky. "You too, sir."

She closed the door, her back against it as she looked at Kenji.

He could see the turmoil in her. A gamut of human emotion played across her face. Anger, frustration, fear, sorrow.

"Are you okay?" he asked.

She didn't answer, but the wetness of her eyes said it all.

The Tantric moment had passed, yet there was tension in the air he could not break. A moment ago he would have joined with her, one being free of desire as she had said. Now they were in separate worlds, a confused warlord and a tearful goddess, broken by the will of an undisciplined man. Sun Ki Han would have taken her without the passion she needed to be truly fulfilled. He understood what she was saying about sex, that without the right motivation, it was nothing more than animal lust, never what she promised.

But sex is not the only way a man and a woman can join. He sensed the anger in her, the hurt, as if he were already a part of her. She glanced up into his eyes, a look that tried to apologize for what just happened.

"It's not your fault," he said. He reached out and she started to cry, falling into his arms like a tree before the woodsman's ax. As he caught her he realized that they were already one being, joined by desire but fused by the single urge to help one another, lovers of a higher order.

He tried to give a name to the stirrings in his heart, as if a fire had been doused with water, yet the flames continued to burn. In this rare moment Kenji Alamoto was not thinking of his people, or himself, he was thinking of only one person.

His arms held her, tight and supportive, his hand instinctively going to the back of her head to pet her gently. "He's gone," he said. "Everything's going to be okay."

She pulled back. "Do you think he would have killed us?"

"He was after me," said Kenji. "You, he loves. He never stopped loving you. He talked about you incessantly on the plane ride here. It fueled my want to meet you." He cradled her head ever so gently. "And now that I have met you, I don't want to let go of you either."

16

Rothschild paced, seething, a drink in his hand. *We're wasting our time here*, he thought. *It's time to play the General card. Get Whiteweather to bring his teams in here and pick this place apart piece by piece. We'll get what we want, one way or the other.* He took another sip of his drink and stepped out onto the balcony. The sun was low in the Western sky, a beautiful sight to any man, but instead he stared into the bottom of his empty glass, thinking about how his dreams were melting away before his eyes.

He and his family had ruled the world from behind the scenes. Banded with a clever bunch of men, long ago they had combined their fortunes and rigged the system to their advantage. Once the scales began to tip, the money and power poured into their laps and from there the rest was easy. A tweak here, a push there, necessary at times and often brutal and Machiavellian in their execution, but these are the types of decisions that men in power must make.

He had inherited this system from his father who inherited it from his father and so on back into the early nineteen hundreds when the post industrial age and capitalism were in their infancy. It had taken a century or more of manipulation to get it right. The United States was the hard part. It took decades of effort against a people brought up on the ideals of freedom. Their spirit had to be broken. But it was the final strategy that destroyed the great nation. Using an old scheme of divide and conquer was the last nail in the coffin. Once the country was divided politically, engaged in social debate, constant demonstrations, even violence, it was easy to manipulate, feeding each faction with half truths and fake news. The citizens were so busy fighting each other that they didn't even notice that their freedom was being siphoned off as quickly as their money, directed into the hands of a few who had, like himself, inherited this system from their fathers. Fear made the people want a stronger police force. With that the reigns of control drew ever tighter. It relentlessly continued, through legislation, rigged elections, bought favors, and through force, until after many years a generation of coddled children grew up to be silent, complacent dummies more interested in pop stars and the media than their government.

Intentional communities like this Village of the Sun survived all that. They were founded, like America, on idealistic principles, often humanistic and spiritual. This kind of world attracted the visionary and the creative. The things they had accomplished were remarkable, and T. Morgan Rothschild knew that he could do the same if he wanted to. But crystal houses and free food were not his goals.

There was a knock at the door. He took his time, fixed himself another drink and braced himself for today's meeting. They knocked again. On the third he opened the door. Chase and Van Dorn stood there, Van Dorn still wearing a silly grin that had been pasted on his face since the hospital visit.

Rothschild grunted and stuck his head out in the hallway looking both ways. "You're here. Haven't seen the rest of the crew, have you?" he said.

"The General is M.I.A. and Kenji said something about having a headache and retiring early," said Chase.

"I'm here, sir," said Van Dorn, his voice squeaky and light.

"What little of you there is," said Rothschild. "You're all doped up like a drug addict. Better come inside." He motioned them in, let them pass and again stuck his head out in the hall. He looked both ways seeing empty corridors. He shut the door, locking it, feeling secure and confident. "What about the rest of them? Any word?"

"The Cardinal went to mass, I imagine to pray for our success. Why did we bring him along anyway?"

"Authenticity," said Rothschild. "Makes us look like a peace mission."

"I haven't seen your publicist, but then, she's not a member of this little group, is she?"

"No, she's not," said Rothschild. "But she hasn't reported in either. I haven't seen her since her doctor's visit."

Van Dorn chimed up for no reason. Childlike, he said, "The doctor put a crystal beside my face and shined a light in my eye." It came out sounding like a school yard admission of superiority.

"And what did that do?" asked Chase.

"I don't know, but it made me feel better," said Van Dorn. "Maybe you should try it."

Rothschild shook his head, spoke to Chase. "How about a drink instead?"

"I could use one," said Chase. "He's been boring me for the last half hour going on about a swim he took this afternoon."

"It was a sacred swim," said Van Dorn.

"See what I mean?" said Chase.

"I wish you could have been there," said Van Dorn. "Both of you."

"Go ahead," said Chase. "Tell Morgan here about the dolphins. I know you want to."

Van Dorn's face lit up, talking like a kid who had caught the prize trophy on a fishing trip. "Barclay McKenner took me on a boat ride. We're less than a half a mile offshore when he stops the boat and tells me to jump in the water. I think, he's going to abandon me, one less committee member to deal with, but instead he takes a megaphone, sticks it in the water, and makes a few odd noises.

Rothschild shrugged and handed a drink to Chase. "Whatever. These people are weird."

"Hold on," said Chase. "He's getting to the best part. Go on, Franklin."

Van Dorn continued. "This dolphin shows up. I think he was a pet because Barclay knew him, introduced him as Neptune. I'm hesitant, bobbing there in the water, and this dolphin starts tapping me with his nose, making all those cute dolphin noises like they do. I'm thinking he wants a fish or something so I swim back towards the boat. Before I can get back in the boat, McKennor jumps overboard. I look around and there's three more of these fish in the water with us."

"I keep telling you. A dolphin is not a fish. It's a mammal," said Chase.

"Whatever," said Van Dorn. "So, the dolphin start squeaking, all four of them. The sounds penetrate my body, it's like I'm feeling the noise inside me. High frequency changes, I feel lighter, happier. I suddenly trust these guys. They have natural smiles. Barclay shows me how to grab their top fin and catch a ride. Geez, I never went so fast underwater. Before I know it I'm having fun like a kid again."

"Weren't you afraid of sharks?" asked Rothschild.

114

"Dolphin and sharks are natural enemies. They would have protected us," said Van Dorn. "Let me finish my story here."

"Let me finish it for you," said Rothschild.

"Why do you do that?" asked Van Dorn. "Belittle me and my experience."

"Because you're crazy right now," said Rothschild. "A flashlight and a crystal couldn't have done this to you man. I don't know what they did to you, but something happened. I wish you'd never seen that doctor. "

"Funny, I feel just the opposite," said Van Dorn. "That doctor did me a favor, cured me of my chest pains. I never felt lighter and happier in my life. Barclay said the dolphins helped too. He said Neptune was a highly evolved ocean teacher. "

"Franklin may be on to something here," said Chase. "The Navy has been trying to weaponize dolphin for years. This could be a breakthrough for us."

"They were just trained pets," said Rothschild.

"These were not pets. Ocean teachers," insisted Van Dorn. "Spiritual guides. They energized my chakras and introduced me to higher realms and dimensions. Did you know that we live in a sea of emotions?"

"Enough about swimming with the fish!" said Rothschild angrily. "I'm tired of hearing about it. You're beginning to sound like them. Let's go to the balcony and talk about something different."

Chase used the electronic scanner to check the room for bugs. It easily passed by the invisible, astral form of Cameron Singh who sat on the couch listening to everything. Chase finished scanning, a determined nod telling Rothschild that they were secure and ready for their private meeting.

They went to the balcony where they took seats, oblivious to astral Singh on a nearby deck chair. Chase put the scanner away and took the jamming device out of his pocket, set it on the table and activated it. Van Dorn took a deep breath and smiled as he sat down. "Oh, Goody," he said. Sunset on the veranda."

Rothschild sneered. "Maybe you'll see some of your dolphin friends in the lagoon."

"You think so?" asked Van Dorn excitedly.

Rothschild put a finger to his temple, making a small circle, the universal sign for crazy. "Just ignore him," he said.

"He's right about something," said Chase,. "It is a pretty sunset."

Rothschild grunted. "That reminds me. Did you hear that Sun was arrested a little while ago?"

"No!" said Chase.

"Some kind of stalking charge," said Rothschild. "They accused him of negative energy or some rot like that. It wasn't even worth calling my lawyers. They're going to release him within the hour."

"What's the penalty?" asked Chase.

"No penalty," said Rothschild. "He's lucky. They caught him with a knife, said he was after his ex-wife. I don't think we can count on him anymore. It's up to us to see this through."

"What about the General?" asked Chase.

"He's my ace in the hole," said Rothschild. "But I'd rather do this the easy way than the hard way. Tell me something good, Van Dorn. Did you get a look inside their power plant last night?"

"Looked pretty normal to me," said Van Dorn. "Nice building, small for a power plant. Pretty artwork. No alien devices or weird apparatus. Their secret is giant batteries for storing power. They collect solar, wind, hydroelectric, and wave action."

"Wave action?" asked Chase.

"Somehow they use the tides," said Van Dorn. "I remember something like that being researched in Seattle."

"I remember it too," said Rothschild. "Another alternative energy source we worked hard to shut down. Gasoline and oil provide all the energy we need."

"Until we run out," said Van Dorn. "And, by the way, you didn't shut it down. The people researching tidal energy just moved here where they could finish their work and put it into practice."

"Damn. Is that so?" said Rothschild. He let out a low hiss. "We have to fight this at the source, shut this place down before it gets worse. Any word from the General about their defenses? Is it time to call in an airstrike?"

"A nuke would do it," said Chase.

"We want a peaceful takeover, Chase," said Rothschild. "If we nuke this place we lose the technology along with the advances these people have made. I expect they're like cattle, easy to pen and enslave."

"From what I can see their defenses are minimal," said Chase. "They have no guns or weapons. Why don't we just march in here with the army?"

"Because they're protected by angels," said Van Dorn.

Rothschild grunted and laughed.

"Right," said Chase. "Since when do you believe in angels?"

"I've always believed in angels," said Van Dorn.

"Why didn't I know this before?" asked Rothschild.

"I guess it never came up. It's not like you asked it on my job application," said Van Dorn. "You believe in angels, don't you?"

"Oh, yeah. And fairies and goblins, too," said Rothschild.

Chase answered snidely. "Right."

"There you go again," said Van Dorn. "Belittling my experience."

Chase ignored him, turned to Rothschild and said, "You'll be happy to know the death toll is climbing logarithmically. We doubled yesterday's numbers almost hitting thirty five million today."

Van Dorn looked sad. "Thirty five million. That's a lot of people. We should do something about that."

"Four days ago you were ready to wipe these people out just to get the secret of their power plants," said Rothschild. "Now all you want to do is help? What did they do to you man?"

"For one thing, they made me appreciate this sunset," said Van Dorn. "End of another day as God draws the curtain down. Beautiful, isn't it?" His demeanor turned, becoming doleful and childlike. "Makes it kind of sad when so many people died today. We could stop this tomorrow. Let's take their deal. End the suffering."

Rothschild was irritated and forceful. "We are not here to take their deal. We're here to get our deal, and don't you forget it." He turned to Chase. "This place is affecting members of the team. I hope you're not next."

"No way," said Chase, looking guilty for enjoying the sunset.

"Good," said Rothschild. "We have to put this to bed. Leave this place before we all turn into mindless, veggie eating dipsticks."

17

The police station, if it could be called that, was a nondescript building off the main street that ran through the center of the village. Kransky escorted Sun to an admitting desk and sat him down. Sun rubbed his arm where the tall man had maintained a constant grip. Kransky sprayed something in Sun's face, a mist from a small bottle. Sun squinted, smelled an odd floral smell and shook his head. "What was that?" he asked.

"Wait here," came the reply. Officer Kransky turned and moved towards an evidence box in the corner of the room, a robotic device that took pictures for the record. He lifted a lid and dropped the knife into the large metallic box. A screen lit up on the wall displaying two options: "DESTROY" or "STORE FOR EVIDENCE". He chose DESTROY and went back to Sun.

"What now, cowboy, I get fingerprinted and jailed?" asked Sun.

"Not quite," said Kransky. "No fingerprints. Just this." Before Sun could react he took a snip of hair from him.

"What's that for?" asked Sun.

"The DNA analysis."

"Had it done through that website on the internet," said Sun. "I'm from Mongolian stock."

Kransky smiled. "We know who you are, Sun Ki Han. We know your past. We're here to help you with your future."

"Right," said Sun.

"Sit tight," said Kransky. "I'll see if a counselor is available."

"Councilor?" asked Sun. "As in a lawyer?"

"More like a life coach," said Kransky. "Just sit here and wait. I'll be back for you."

He walked off, across the room towards an ornate, carved door with a small window in the center. Sun saw the tall man flash a badge that opened it, watched the massive door close behind him. His thoughts drifted. He looked around. *This is not what a police station should look like*, he thought. The room was large, a high ceiling overhead. The walls were not unlike some he had seen in Rothschild's mansion, elegant and wainscoted, the upper half painted white, the bottom rich, paneled wood. To one side was a mural, the bright colors leaping off the wall like insects on a summer night. He assumed a row of doors along another wall led to offices.

Other than him the station was empty. He was the only one in the room. A brisk walk down a short corridor lay between him and his freedom. He scanned the office again and casually got up, heading towards the corridor. Two steps into it he had a reaction, an intense urge to vomit. He doubled over, dry heaving, wondering what he had for dinner and why it was coming up now. A man came out of one of the offices, an air sickness bag in his hand. He gave it to Sun.

"Here. Don't mess up the floor," he said. "And stay away from the door. Didn't Officer Kransky tell you to sit over there and wait?"

He helped Sun back to his seat. "Thank you," he said between heavy breaths. "How'd you know I was puking?"

"I saw you, not that I couldn't hear you retching like a drunk old man."

Sun looked around. "Video monitor?"

"Nah," said the man. He pointed towards his office. "One way walls. I see out but you don't see in." He smiled. "I'm Chief Wiggins, head man here. You're from the outside world, aren't you?"

Sun nodded.

"What did you do to land you in the Peace Station?" asked the Chief.

"I'm innocent," said Sun. "I was framed."

The Chief laughed. "Sure. Sure."

Sun was belligerent. "Look. Quit the talk, Pops. Just take me to my cell."

"Can't do that," said the Chief. "We don't have holding cells. Since this is your first time here, let me show you around."

"It's okay," said Sun. "I've been around a police station."

Chief Wiggins snickered. "I bet you have. Pretty hardened criminal, are you?"

"Is that what your cop sense tells you?" asked Sun.

"Now you're thinking," said the Chief. "Yes. I have a *cop sense* about you. You're all hurt inside so you're going to take it out on the world. Make other people suffer like you are. Am I right so far?"

"So what if you are?" said Sun.

"Then I'm guessing you'll either be full of pride and ego and support this new criminal image of yourself," said the Chief. "Or you'll wake up and see what's really going on here. You're on a downward spiral."

Kransky returned. "The Councilor is ready for you," he said.

"Who is he seeing?" asked Wiggins.

Kransky smiled like Christmas. "Monica."

The Chief nodded, turned toward Sun. "You're lucky. She'll cure you for sure, or at least set you in the right direction." He clapped Sun on the back. "Good luck."

Sun felt Kransky's grip on his arm again, squeezing it like it held the last precious drops of orange juice or something. "This way," he said.

They went through the ornate door, then through another door into a into a long, rectangular room. It was low lit and he had trouble making out what lay at the other end. Kransky plopped him down on a chair. "Have a seat. The Counselor will be with you in a moment," he said. Then he turned and quickly exited the room.

There was total silence as Sun studied the surroundings. A light above the chair flashed at regular intervals, cycling through a spectrum of colors. Some made him squint and retract, shielding his eyes. Other colors seemed to soothe him. Finally the light held steady on a soft, green hue, shining bright and even. At the distal end of the room, lighting slowly illuminated a figure, a beautiful woman sitting in a chair behind a desk. Sun did not see her in the relative darkness. She studied him with interest, making notes on a tablet. She pressed a button on a remote control and a table near Sun lit up.

He was drawn to it. There were a variety of objects on the table, among them the knife he had on him when he was arrested outside Kenji's room. Sun went to grab it but found it was a phantom, a holographic image that only looked real. Monica spoke from the other side of the room, breaking the silence, her voice strong and commanding.

"Why did you reach for the knife?" she asked.

"Impulse," he said. "Besides, it was the only object that I recognized."

"There's also a prayer book, a candle, a set of keys, and money," she said. "You don't recognize these things?"

"I was getting around to it. I would have gone for the money next," he said, sounding like a teenage hoodlum defending his turf.

"I see," she said calmly. "Your choice represents a selfish, security driven need, but I sense something else in you."

"My charisma?" he asked, trying to sound charming.

She tapped the finger of one hand in the palm of the other making strange sounds, chirping like a bird a few times. "What's that you say?" she asked. "Do you think..."

"I said, *my charisma*," he repeated.

Her response was quick. "Quiet, I wasn't talking to you."

Sun was disappointed. "Oh." was all he could muster. *Then who the hell is she talking to*, he thought. He looked around the empty room. The holographic table caught his eye again. He walked over

124

to it, swiping at the images on the table, trying to grab the money first. He continued to hear her talking in the background. "Hmmmm. Third party negative entity?" he heard her say.

He smirked and rolled his eyes. He went back to the table and tried to pick up the holographic knife. When he couldn't even touch it, he made a gesture across his wrists with an invisible knife like he wanted to slit them, rolling his eyes again at Monica. *You're just another crazy lady talking to her invisible friends,* he thought.

Monica observed this behavior but continued her conversation. "I know," she said. "I read his thoughts too."

He turned around and studied her. She had dark hair and dark eyes, the kind that followed you around the room no matter where you moved. She wasn't watching him, instead she stared into empty space, what looked like a blank wall in the semi-darkness. Who was she talking to? He looked around the room wondering if there were people he couldn't see hidden in the darkness, maybe another one way wall.

Bored with watching her go on, he turned his back to her, looking again for the table. It was gone. He ran his hand through the air in front of him, trying to feel for it, but there was nothing.

"Can I request a reader?" he heard her say. There was a pause while she waited for whatever it is she requested.

"My ex-wife Nan used to do that," he said.

"What?" she asked.

"Look at you, all high and mighty, just like her," he said. "Talking to your invisible friends."

"You think just because I'm spiritual I don't have pain in my life?" she said. "You have no idea, Mister. I lost my husband when I ascended and began to talk to my *invisible friends*."

"So did she," he said. "I got tired of the competition. She spent more time with them than with me."

"Did it hurt your ego?" she asked. "You seem to be the one suffering, not her."

Sun snorted. "What did your invisible friends say about me?"

"You really want our input?" she asked.

"No!" he snorted. "Not really."

"Well you're going to get it anyway, because we have information for you and I'm not going to hold it back. You have a multitude of emotions you can't understand. You're jealous over Nan. You admire this place, this community. It appeals to you, and you marvel at what she has accomplished here professionally. Her skills and knowledge of agriculture have revolutionized food production here. You wonder what you could have done in her place."

He sat back into the chair, stunned with her report on him. Every word was true, down to the deepest feelings he had hidden, even from himself, for all these years.

"You must know, she planted every garden in this Village," she said.

"Every garden?" he asked. "That's impossible."

"Oh, of course she had help. Everyone wanted to work with her. But she directed the plantings, the species, their locations, even the tiers and the designs of the gardens. She built communities of plants the way we built communities of people."

126

Sun sat in silence, waiting for what was next. Her finger tapped in her palm.

"A long time ago you had an opportunity to move to this Village with her, start a family, but you chose another path. Your path was not as fortunate, and instead of building your spiritual bridge, you made dark commitments to men in power. Then, to compensate your guilt, you staged an elaborate and excessive lifestyle."

Right on target.

"Now you feel lost, another emotion in a mix so thick, it's hard for you to see your way out of it. But there's a deeper problem here, something linked to all of the above. You've been infected with third party negative energy."

"Third party negative energy?" he asked. "What the hell is that?"

"Hell is exactly what it is," she said, her voice softening. "Come here, sit on this stool by my desk."

A stool lit up in the middle of the long room and Monica came out from behind her desk to meet him halfway. Sun was hesitant. "I don't bite," she said. "But I will warn you. I'm an expert in karate and well practiced in aikido. Try anything and I'll cripple you in a way that you won't bother anyone ever again. But we're not here to fight, are we? We're here for help." She looked off to the side of him, her voice softening even more. "Don't be afraid, help has arrived, your angelic team is here."

Sun meekly approached the stool. "Angelic team?" he asked.

"Yes. Angels," she said. "You believe in them, don't you?"

"Yes. I used to," he said. "My mother told me I had a guardian angel."

"Yes. Everybody has a guardian angel," she said. "Yours has been through hell with you. No wonder you're miserable. Do you ever pray?"

"When I was a kid," he said. "My prayers were never answered."

"You prayed for material things," she said, her voice even and sure.

"I guess so," he said.

"Did you do anything to try to make them happen?"

He looked away from her. "I guess not," he said.

"You have..." she trailed off, looking at the blank wall again, her finger pressed into the palm of her hand. "One, two, three. Three. Three angels around you. Two have been busy fighting the third party negative energies that have taken up residence inside you. We're going to remedy that. Sit on the stool. Tell me about your mother."

She touched his shoulder as he sat, delivering a psychic tranquilizer. He grew visibly calmer, beginning to sift through memories about his mother.

"My mother was a beautiful woman," he said. "I was an only child and got all her attention. She taught me to read, told me stories, and gave me my life skills."

Her finger twitched in her palm. "And your father was just the opposite."

Unmistakable sadness clouded his face, eclipsed with hatred. "He had anger issues. He was mean and beat her."

The finger twitched again. "He assumed she was infertile and barren. You were the only child. He wanted many sons."

"I never knew that," said Sun. His eyes widened, focusing like binoculars on his distant past. "He beat me too."

"He wanted you to be mean to your mother, to look down at all women, but you couldn't do that, could you?"

"No!"

"He accused you of being a mamma's boy." She slapped her hands together, extended them straight out. She closed her eyes, whispering. "I ground myself, deep into the center of the Earth, I am safe. I am secure. I center myself in my heart, I am love, loving, and beloved. I connect to my Higher Self and I am receiving Divine energy." She began rubbing her hands together, a dynamo of psychic energy building between her palms.

Sun was fearful. "What are you doing?"

She spoke aloud in her commanding voice again, looking out and beyond him into some vastness he could not fathom. "I'm asking for a blessing, filling this room with White Light. I ask this in Jesus' name, clear the room please, all the Lords and angels present. Angels of protection in four corners, Guardians bless us, keep evil at bay while we help Sun Ki."

Before he could react she approached him, stretching her hands out as she placed one on his back and the other on his navel. He felt something move inside, that was as close as he could describe it. "Clearing chakras, pushing the negative energy away. Leave! You've been exposed. Va! Va! Go to an appropriate place! No longer wanted here."

She pulled at something invisible inside him, stretching it out of his body, as if peeling away elastic. He could feel it gripping his innards. He started to twitch.

"Stay still," she commanded. He obeyed but he still felt something pulling at his guts.

He let out a cry, bending forward as she released him. "Ahhh!"

The tension was over. She made a gesture as if pushing something away with her hands.

"We managed to get one out of you," she said. "They're taking it away to an appropriate place."

"What?" said Sun.

"There's one more," she said. "This one's a little harder, dug in pretty deep. We're going to rest a minute before we get that one. How do you feel?"

He breathed deep. "Not so angry anymore." He looked up at her respectfully. The urge to ridicule her seemed to leave with the dark elastic.

"Keep breathing," she said. "I'm going to clear your heart chakra and then we're going to get that other negative entity out of you."

"Yes," said Sun. "The third party negative energy. You said that before. Does it mean what I think it means?"

"You might call it a demon," she said. "This one attached itself to you when you were very young. You got it from your father. My guides tell me he was a repository for negative entities."

His mouth hung open. "Demon possession? By my father?"

"It was not your fault. You were six at the time, almost seven." she said. She glanced at the wall, something there catching her attention. "Okay, it's time." She began to charge up again, rubbing her hands together to gather and concentrate prana, the mystic healing energy that we take in with each breath. She placed her hands around him, starting at the throat, placing them gently over his chakras and clearing them. As she did, he started to talk, something that usually happened as people released karma from the past alongside negative entities.

"It makes sense now," he said. "He cornered me one day. I thought he was going to beat me again but he leaned in close. I'll never forget his eyes, it was like staring into pools of darkness. He leaned in real close and said, *One day you're going to meet the devil. And when you do, give him this.* His breath smelled of alcohol and he opened wide and exhaled on me. It was like a roar of wind. I coughed, inhaled in a spasm and started to choke. He slapped me on the back and said *Swallow hard! Suck it up. Be a man. Get a taste of what I have to deal with.*"

Monica nodded, compassion and understanding reflected in her eyes. "Do you suffer from depression?"

"All the time," he said. "I hate my life."

"Let's see if we can change that." She closed her eyes, raised her arms and for the first time Sun noticed that the room was not dark at all, It was actually filled with bright, White light.

18

The morning was never brighter for the guests assembled in the Grand Dining Room at the Reiki Spa and Resort. An elaborate array of windows provided a beautiful view of the city. The color of autumn corn glowed as the sun slowly rose over the crystal mountain, reflecting a pattern that could only be created by nature. Rays of light seemed to pierce the water in the lagoon and illuminate every drop in every wave.

The great room contained a single, long table made of carved wood. It held a feast of fruits and vegetables, dishes carved into exotic shapes, as appealing to the eye as the palate. Servers pleasantly refilled glasses with fresh juice squeezed from a juicing station by the wall. Members of the Think Tank sat at the table, mixed in with their new friends, the visiting dignitaries. Chef Aaron was beside the General chatting at one end of the table, the container of Nirvana Pie resting in front of him. Juliana was next to him, boisterously adding to the conversation with her laughter. A few empty chairs lie between them where Van Dorn perched between Baba Randall and Barclay McKenner. Further down the table Cameron Singh bent low over the table speaking to Chase in a quiet voice.

Juliana let out another peal of laughter. Everyone around her was jovial and full of smiles. Randall leaned forward, casting a grin in her direction. At the other end of the table, Singh and Chase did not seem to notice. They continued to speak, their conversation kept low and quiet.

"Where is the Cardinal this morning?" asked Chef Aaron. "I really wanted to meet him."

"I think you will, Aaron," said Juliana. "He's decided to stay here for a while."

"Is that so?" mused the General. "What made him decide to do that?"

"Singh told me he wanted to study religion," said Juliana.

"But he's a priest, a Cardinal in the Catholic Church at that," said the General.

"He's had an awakening," explained Juliana. "He's hungry to learn about all religions, not just the one he belongs to, but all of them. Singh convinced him that this is the best place in the world for that since we have representation of all religions. Unlike book learning, he can attend services here and see how the people practice their faith. It's much more personal than studying it in the seminary."

"By God, that's good news," said the General. "Cardinal Jameson was complaining on the plane trip here. Said he had lost touch with God, that the Church had become more of a business than a house of worship. Said he spent more time counting the collection plate than saving souls."

"Maybe he's found his humanity again," said Juliana.

"What about Rothschild? Where's he?" asked Aaron. "I wanted him to try a piece of my pie."

"Rothschild dines alone in his room," said the General. "We're just the hired help."

Aaron looked quizzical. "Hired help? Really? Is that how you think of yourself? If you don't mind me asking, what's he paying you?"

"Rothschild pays in favor, not money," said the General. "He promised to launch me into the Presidency. There hasn't been a military man in the White House since Eisenhower." He looked over at Juliana and smiled. "I'm not sure I want that anymore."

"Why?" asked Juliana "I thought it was every boy's dream to grow up to be President."

"Oh, I wouldn't say no to the job, it's just what he wanted me to do after I took office," said the General.

"What's that?" asked Aaron.

The General let out a puff of air. "Rothschild wants to rule the world. America stands in the way of that. He's been pecking at the soul of our nation for years, trying to bring us down. He's using the old divide and conquer strategy, buying up the media and spreading lies and rumors. He's got us fighting each other. But I see that turning around. America is coming together again. We're at our best when the world is at its worst. This disaster, as terrible as it is, may be just what we need to come together and help each other."

Kenji and Nan entered from the far side of the room. She wore a flowing dress, the fabric surrounding her like the petals of a flower. She smiled, moving towards the table as the General flagged them over. He rose gallantly as Nan arrived, offering her an empty chair.

Kenji bowed ceremoniously as he pulled the chair out to seat her. "Good morning Carson," he said. "How are you this morning? Juliana?"

They both nodded and smiled as Kenji took a seat.

Juliana made quick introductions. "Kenji, Nan, this is Chef Aaron. He's made a unique desert I think you should try."

"Aaron and I have met," said Nan. She looked at Kenji. "I would definitely recommend the dessert," she said.

Alamoto smiled like a kid. "Then maybe I should skip the main course and go right for the sweets." He romantically touched Nan's cheek, indicating that she was his sweet. A blush of color flashed across her face as she looked down at the table. Juliana smiled, letting Nan know that her reaction did not go unnoticed.

Chef Aaron wasted no time. He sliced a thin piece of Nirvana Pie and placed it on a plate in front of him. Kenji looked at it but went on talking to Carson. "And what did you do last night, my friend?"

The General looked hesitatingly at Juliana and smiled. "I went to heaven last night."

Kenji mirrored his smile, wide and full of teeth. He looked over at Nan. "So did I! So did I."

Aaron, Juliana and the General laughed.

Further down the table, Randall turned, his ear taking in the laughter and adding a sparkle to his eyes. He turned back towards Van Dorn who also had a smile.

"Laughter is really the best medicine," said Franklin. "I mean, your doctor helped, but I think I know what that means now." He laughed, a moment of introspection before he added, "I can laugh like a dolphin."

"It's been good hearing about your experience with Neptune and her pod of dolphin," said Randall. "I'm just sorry you didn't get to meet Joan Ocean when she was here. She started this whole program after she realized that dolphin were highly advanced, spiritual beings."

"Where is Joan now?" asked Van Dorn.

Barclay answered. "Hawaii, where her work started. I have a copy of her book. You might be interested in it. *Dolphins into the Future*."

"Dolphin are our counterparts in the sea," said Randall. "Our two species, working together, can change the world."

"Why don't we all have a swim after breakfast?" suggested Barclay.

At the far end of the table, Chase Rockefeller and Cameron Singh sat away from the others. They had their heads together, bent over their plates, speaking in low tones.

"So we agree," said Singh. "I will provide you with a small, working model of a triflux generator."

"The ultimate power," said Chase, his voice hushed, as if revering a God.

"Yes!" said Singh. "And in return you will give me...?" He let the fragment hang, waiting for it to fill with Chase's imagination.

"Riches beyond your dreams," he said. "Rothschild will pay a fortune for it. I'll split the money with you. You'll have enough to buy a private island anywhere in the world. Start your own community, village, country, whatever you want."

"Then we have a deal."

Singh smiled, the glint in his eye emitting a bright light as he focused his attention on another version of himself. He was sitting beside Mel and Stine in the conference room. His body shimmered with astral energy, not corporeal or physical, but as real as anything. When he spoke, his friends heard him in a clear and strong voice. "He took the bait."

Mel smiled. "Then I better get a Triflux generator ready for him."

"Does he even know what a Triflux generator is?" asked Stine.

"Only that it's the ultimate power source," said Singh.

"It is!" said Mel. "It's a meditation tool that connects you with God by generating certain wavelengths of energy. God is the ultimate power."

"What's he going to do when he finds out it doesn't create electricity?" asked Stine.

"I guess he'll figure it out," said Singh. "If he turns it on enough, he'll evolve, maybe embrace meditation and become a better person."

"Won't that be nice," said Stine.

"You need to start the preparations," said Singh. "The relief effort begins within the hour."

"I'm going to wait for approval from Baba," said Mel.

"You're wasting time," said Singh. "The flotilla needs to leave tonight. I'm attending a meeting in New Maya, City of Worlds right now, too."

Stine got up, astonished. He went over to a monitor in the corner, the words "New Maya City of Worlds" in block letters across the bottom of the screen. Cameron Singh sat at the end of a table, waving at him from the monitor. He turned back to Singh, seated at the table. "New Maya agrees with me. They're loading up airships

137

as I speak. They are anxious to give the world hope, even if they have to violate international law and send relief without being invited. As they see it, the political collapse of the world is imminent. There is no government to deal with. The people don't see it yet, but the power has fallen back into their hands, not the politicians."

"I'm not so sure, Singh," said Mel.

"Listen, I'll make a bet with you," said Singh.

"Don't bet with him, Mel," said Stine. "He knows the timeline, probably from some future version of himself."

There was a sigh of victory from an astral body that doesn't breathe.

"I guess he's right," said Mel. "I'll give the order. Fuel the airships. We'll take the food out of storage and start loading it aboard. We could be ready to go by this afternoon or early evening if I cheat and use antigravity."

Stine looked off into the distance, "I better get ready analyzing data, planning sites for water wells and villages. Where do I start?"

"Africa first, my friend," said Singh. "Kenji Alamoto is anxious to save his people. Then America. Whiteweather says he doesn't need approval. Marshall Law is in effect. He's taking over until order is restored. Once we get the support of the United States, the world will follow."

"What about Rothschild?" said Stine. "He's not getting the picture like the others."

"Rothchild's power is eroding. Once we return the resources to the people he'll have nothing to control. He'll have a small, crumbling empire mostly staffed by dark ones and lower entities, but they will be a minority. They'll leave soon, evacuate with a lot of other negative entities. Gaia will have her chance at ascension."

"All right then. I'm in," said Mel. "I'll give the order. Let's get busy."

There was a glint again, a bright sparkle from deep in Singh's eye. His astral form dissolved in front of Mel and Stine and he was transported back to the breakfast table. Chase was going on and on, spinning his dreams like a seven legged spider. "We'll be set for life," he was saying. "I don't know what you're going to do with your half, Singh, but I'm going to..."

He went on and on. Singh was amazed at what Chase was thinking. Materialism was a sickness that infected the rich and the type of people they attract. Anybody in the world can get anything they want if they work hard enough and put their energy into it, but to continue to collect things and accumulate money way beyond your needs borders on obsession. Chase was so wrapped up in his dreams he didn't see Sun Ki Han come through the door at the far side of the room.

It did not escape the General's eye, though. "Uh oh, Kenji," he said. "Sun just showed up. And from what you and Nan just told me there could be trouble."

Sun stopped inside the door and scanned the room. Kenji was just turning around when Sun spotted he and Nan with the General. Sun slowly walked toward them. Kenji started to stand, confrontational, ready for anything. Nan stood up too and it didn't take long for the General to join them. It was Nan who broke the silence. "What do you want, Sun?" she asked pointedly.

Sun looked down, hesitated. His eyes darted around. Randall was aware of what was happening but Singh and Chase continued going about their business. Sun looked at Nan. "I want to apologize," he said, turning towards Kenji. "To you too. To both of you. I don't know what's gotten into me lately." He looked down again and laughed. "No, that's not true. I do know what's gotten into me, but I'm working on it. I really just came here to apologize."

Nan stared into his eyes for the eternity of a moment. "You're sincere. I can tell."

"Then, you forgive me?" he asked.

She reached out and hugged him. His face lit with joy, not lust, spreading across him like a fresh wind tickling the prairie. Tears started to flood his eyes as they parted.

She was also crying. "I never stopped caring about you, Sun, but I don't know if there's any future for us. Let's not go over the past. For now, let me just say, I forgive you." She hugged him one more time, a quick, shallow one, then released him to face Kenji.

"And you?" he asked. "Do you also forgive me?"

Kenji was uncertain. "You're not going to cause any more trouble?"

"I've had enough trouble," said Sun.

Kenji took his hand and shook it firmly, smiling wide enough to show the world all his teeth. "It takes a strong man, a good man, to admit his wrongs and face up to himself. You're a good man, Sun Ki Han. I accept your apology."

"Thank you." Sun turned, a great weight lifted from his soul. There was still an emptiness inside him, once filled with demons. He breathed deep, the ornate door of the Grand Ballroom beckoning like a portal to a new version of himself.

"Wait," said Kenji. "Don't go. Why don't you sit and join us for breakfast? I was about to try a piece of this wonderful pie the General has been touting." He stood aside, pulled out an empty chair and offered it to Sun. The General nodded too, lowering himself beside Juliana again.

Sun turned to decline, but stopped himself before he could speak. He stood for a moment, blinking. He saw them at the table. They were all laughing, glowing with morning sunlight. He felt the emptiness within slowly fill with the warm smiles of acceptance, inviting him to share their bounty of friendship. He took a step, quieting the remaining demons he harbored, belaying their lies about his self worth and the penalties of sin. Each step felt warmer and soon he wore a smile as big as theirs.

"Chef Aaron, would you care to cut another piece of pie?" said the General.

19

Rothschild paced in his room. His breakfast did not set well with him. He had a slight hangover from too much liquor last night and his sweat had the fetid smell of poisons. Caffeine was only making it worse. He sat on the balcony staring out at the placid sea. He checked his watch, wondering what his cronies were up to. He thought about going down to the beach, but he knew he wouldn't be able to relax. This mission was going to hell.

"Am I the only one who sees that?" he said aloud, talking to himself.

No matter which way he turned his way seemed to be blocked. They were going on their third day here and still no progress towards an agreement.

As he looked across the lagoon he saw a boat heading out to sea. Baba Randall was distinct, his cleric robes flapping in the breeze. Next to him was Van Dorn, a stupid grin on his face that was quickly becoming his trademark look these days. Barclay McKenner was at the wheel. For all intent, they looked like they were on vacation. "Don't these people care about the world?"

He answered his own question. "Obviously not. The world is falling apart and they're going boating! That just figures."

A black bird looked at him from a nearby tree. It started calling, "Caw, caw," sounding like laughter or even the toll of a bell.

"Nobody asked you anyway," he grumbled. As if a reply, there was a knock at the door. He got up, flicked his half empty cup of coffee at the bird and it flew away. He set the empty cup down and opened the door. Kenji and the General stood there.

He offered them no greeting. "About time you two showed up. Where you been?" He held the door open but they did not come in.

Kenji spoke first. "I came to say goodbye, Rothschild. I took their deal. I'm headed back to Africa."

Rothschild flared. "Traitor. I'll break you for this," he said. "I'll have you assassinated and replaced."

Alamoto flared back, his face contorting in anger. "Then have me assassinated! Kill me now if you wish, but I've made my decision. My people will have a chance at survival. I've given the order and the plans are underway."

"Have it your way," said Rothschild. He looked at the General, took a step sideways and held the door open. "Come on in, Carson. We have business to discuss. Time for plan B."

The General shook his head. "I'm afraid not. I'm going too, Harmon. I found a loophole. The people of the United States of America have gratefully accepted the offer to help. The President has been deposed, impeached and exiled to the penal colony on Staten Island with the rest of his cabinet."

"That's a lie," said Rothschild.

"Check the news feeds, Harmon," said Whiteweather. "You'll see I'm not lying. My country needs me. I'm headed back today, leaving this afternoon with an armada of relief. I can't wait to see what happens. As the U.S. stabilizes we'll spread to Canada and Europe through the NATO alliance."

Rothschild fumed. "Europe? You wouldn't do that to me, Carson."

The General spoke calmly, his words soft and meaningful. "I'm not doing it to you, Harmon. It's more like I'm doing it for humanity."

"I'll have you stripped of your rank," said Rothschild. "Dishonorably discharged. Publicly humiliated."

"There's nothing you can threaten me with, Rothschild. Nothing. There may not even be an army when I get back. It's chaos out there. I am a military man, used to performing under pressure, critical decisions, life and death on the scale every day. But this is a different kind of battle, Harmon. The world needs me, needs us. Hell come in on this with us. Look what Eighth Day Village and New Maya have done for Mexico. They were the first to accept help and this country is thriving, no death, no starvation, everyone grateful. A mass of spirituality has overcome the population as a result. They thank God for being spared. The churches are full again. Look, Harmon, I'm clear on this. I've been enlightened. What do you say? It's time to fold and go home."

"No way." Rothschild slammed the door, rubbed his forehead and shook his head in disbelief. He went to the bathroom and took a bottle of pills out of his travel kit, swallowed a few, and looked in the mirror. His face was hard, his resolve firm. There was a bottle of liquor on the counter. He poured a drink and slugged it down, medicine for his aching brain.

"No one pushes T. Harmon Rothschild around and gets away with it," he said. "Nobody."

Outside the door. Kenji and the General looked at each other and smiled as they turned and walked down the corridor. "Hard, but it was the right thing to do," said Kenji.

"Yeah. But that felt good," said Carson.

"Not half as good as what we're about to do," said Kenji.

They rounded the corner where they were met by Juliana and Nan.

Nan wrapped her arms around Alamoto. "I heard what you just said. By something good, did you mean, spend time with us?"

"I meant saving the world, but I must admit, doing it with you at my side makes it twice as pleasurable."

The General pulled Juliana close, hugged her and gave her a kiss. "How about you, High Priestess. You coming to America with me?"

She kissed him back. Passionately. "Wouldn't miss it for the world, farm boy."

20

Baba Randall stared at the screen and smiled. For a lifetime he had dreamed of this moment. His vision of intentional communities was spreading to the world. On one monitor he saw his visionary brothers and sisters in New Maya City of Worlds busily loading airships with supplies. Huge airships the size of redwoods, carved and loaded with supplies for a hungry and waiting world. Thick jungle vines tethered the massive, hollow trees to airbags that offset the weight, even laden as they were.

General Carson Whiteweather got up from the conference table behind Randall leaving Mel and Darius in deep conversation. Moving to his side, he gently put his hand on Randall's shoulder. "I don't know how we can ever thank you," he said.

"I was thinking the same thing," said Randall. "I don't know how I can ever thank you. For all your help."

"What? Reviewing lists and bills of laden? Helping with the logistics? Doing what comes natural to a man with my skills?"

"And we are glad to have them," said Randall. "No, I was thinking about your help in making an old man's dream come true. It has taken a lifetime of work to get to this point. Oh, there have been intentional communities in the past, but nothing on the scale of Eighth Day Village or New Maya. It is only by our sheer size and mass that we are able to mount this relief effort."

146

"I'm amazed at how many of your citizens volunteered to help," said Whiteweather.

"They all would go if we let them, but many are needed here to sustain our presence, to continue to meet our needs as well as the world's."

Ravi entered the conference room, going directly to Randall. "The arrangements have been made, Baba. Juliania and Nan have their export visas, travel documents, and itineraries." He turned to the men seated at the table. "Doctor McKenner, here are the documents for your trip to America. And here are yours, Mel. You and Doctor Stine are going to Africa." He handed them all packets.

Mel opened his and inspected the contents. Randall came over and stood behind him looking over his shoulder. "I'm sorry to lose you for a while," he said.

"This is a massive operation," said Mel. "The logistics are staggering."

"At least we have the help of our sister village, New Maya City of Worlds," said Barclay. "They have offered to send teachers, laborers, and spiritual advisers. They will rendezvous with our flotilla after liftoff. The rest is up to you."

"I've ordered entertainers as well," said Mel. "Musicians who want to perform for the people and raise their spirits with music."

"I'm sure they'll be joined by the locals," said Randall. "Africa is resplendent with song and music."

Stine shook his hand as Mel got up. "Good luck, then, Mel. I'll join you in a few days after I finish up what I'm doing here."

"Good. I will have need of your deep time ecology practices to site these gardens and watering holes. With your help and calculations the new native fauna will have the access they need to return to the land in record numbers."

"You have my first pass at the data," said Stine. "No less than fifty sites. Should keep you busy 'till I get there."

"Wrap things up as quickly as you can," said Randall. "I have the feeling the rest of the world will follow soon. Fifty sites will turn into five hundred, and then five thousand."

"We'd better get busy, then," said Mel. "This is the first of many flotillas. A new hope for humanity."

The astral form of Cameron Singh appeared next to Darius. Carson turned to look at him, then turned back to the monitor. Cameron Singh was standing on a gangplank next to an airship checking off items on a manifest. Carson turned around again and looked at Singh.

"You'll get used to him," said Randall. "He's always popping in and out like that."

"New Maya is ready with Operation Eagle. The ships are being loaded with the supplies requested by the General," said Singh. "The rest of our ships are in the underground hangers on the other side of the mountains being loaded with supplies."

Carson looked at an image on a different screen. Giant wooden dirigibles were floating silently and effortlessly as they skimmed the bottom of low hanging clouds.

"New Maya's fleet," said Randall. "On their way here. They make their airships out of jungle material. Grow a lot of them from trees."

"I don't understand," said Carson. "How do you keep that much weight afloat? Seems like the balloon would need to be ten times the size it is."

Randall leaned in close and whispered. "I'll let you in on a little secret. We cheat and use anti-gravity devices. I can tell you that now that you've joined our community."

Whiteweather nodded and smiled. "I'd like to stay here and really be a part of this but I can't."

"We understand," said Randall. "As long as you continue to meditate daily you'll be in contact with us. And Juliana is going with you I hear."

"To continue teaching me," he said. "And to be my liaison to Gaia."

Darius interrupted. "Our ships are ready to lift off, Baba. On schedule and ready to rendezvous with New Maya."

"So I see," said Randall. They looked into the monitor and saw the Cardinal blessing the fleet. Beside him stood Nan Chi Han and Kenji Alamoto, reverent and thankful. Julie Ann Carver moved around busily snapping pictures and documenting the event.

The overhead hanger doors slowly began to open, pouring light on the massive crystalline ships that lined the floor. One of them came to life, gently rising above the others. As it turned, caught in the sunlight, a light storm of rainbows danced across the hanger bay. Smiles were everywhere, faces lit with refracted color. The Cardinal stood on the dais as the group around him slowly filed down a gangplank and into a nearby crystal ship. Kenji turned and waved and Nan Chi blew kisses to the crowd. As the first ship cleared the overhead door, a second began to lift off.

Behind it cargo was being loaded into the bodies of giant crystals. Grains, supplies, gardening tools, seeds, food, clothing, temporary shelters, solar powered tractors and harvesters, all loaded into massive airships as they prepared for flight. Unlike the wood and vines preferred by New Maya, these ships were designed by Eighth Day engineers and made of crystals as well as native materials. Dirigible balloons hung limp beside the massive remaining crystals, dock workers securing lines and preparing to inflate them. One ship had a giant tank of sea water inside it, dolphin busily directing the storage of supplies as the ship was prepared for flight.

"Is that a tuba I see being loaded into that ship?" asked Carson.

"We're sending musicians to America as well," said Randall. "It elevates the soul and soothes the spirit. Any task is easier when accompanied by the right music."

"Don't I know it," said Carson. "I played cello in my high school band."

"Really?" said Randall. "I preferred drums and percussion. I encourage you to try some of our locally made instruments. We have world class designers here."

"I did, over at the music hall," said the General. "Who could resist playing a crystal cello?" Carson stepped over to another monitor that had a scrolling list of items, amounts, and destinations. He touched the screen, easily narrowing the list to show all the musical instruments on the manifest. "There are far more instruments than people," said Carson.

"Our people volunteered them. We're going to give them away. I'd rather see people making music than out in the streets rioting." He pointed to a nearby screen that was showing the news feed. It was the same story: world chaos, war, panic, and mounting tension.

"If only they knew help was on the way," said Carson.

"We sent word," said Randall. "But Rothschild controls the media. He squelched the story. It doesn't matter. The U.S. relief effort will begin as soon as the African armada leaves. Once they rendezvous with the flotilla arriving from New Maya they'll follow the prevailing winds and head west from here, over the oceans and on to Africa."

"Bringing Light to the Dark Continent," said Carson.

"I've never liked that phrase," said Randall. "The continent never was dark. It was Westerners and colonials that made it so."

"Yes, of course," said Carson. "Well I better get ready."

"Om. Shanti. Ajo!" said Randall.

21

Randall and Darius stood with the crowd on the beach watching the last of the crystal dirigibles float away. His heart felt as light as the ships, as if he himself were on antigravity. Peace came over him, and as he filled his heart with it, he turned it outward, willing it into the world where everyone could enjoy his sense of fulfillment.

"You did it, Randall."

"We did it, Darius," said the Holy Man. "You, me, Stine, even Manny and Vera. We built a community of enlightened beings, and when the world needed us, we were ready."

"What about the world, Randall? We have paradise here. How long before the world realizes it can be like this?"

"Not long at all, Darius," said Singh. "Now that we have the right people working on it."

Van Dorn walked by, a swim mask in his hands. "Where are you off to, Franklin?" asked Randall.

"Full moon swim with the dolphin," he said. "The pod needs me."

"Since when?" asked Darius.

"Since Neptune is gone. I thought you knew. He's up in one of those crystal ships right now headed for Washington D.C. I convinced him to address Congress. He's very concerned about the status of the coral reefs in the U.S. Marine Sanctuaries. ”

“Have a good swim.”

Franklin turned towards the beach, took a step before turning back to face Randall. “Something I've been meaning to ask,” he said. “I've seen your original proposal. Harmon showed it to me, oh, thirty or forty years ago. I remember the title: Free the Giraffes in Mexico. What did you mean by that?”

“Just what it implies,” said Randall. “Yes. It started as just an odd catch phrase, a way of getting people to pick it up and read it, but there are other reasons.”

“Well, that one worked. I read it,” said Van Dorn.

“Well, yes. It started that way, but in the end I found that I like waking up in the morning with a giraffe and a mango smoothie. The giraffe is here because he wants to be here. That's what deep time ecology is all about, animals returning to the continent. All that and I like riding a giraffe down the beach in the morning. We both enjoy it. You should try it some time.”

“No thanks. I think I'll stick to riding dolphins” he said. He gave Randall a pat on the back before moving on.

Randall watched him walk away, a slow mindful gait that touched the sand in a most gentle way. “My how you've changed, Franklin,” he murmured. In the sky the airships had shrunk to tiny dots in the distance. The sun was setting over the lagoon, reflecting across the azure sea. A golden splay of color flashed as it sank into the ocean. In the other direction the moon was peeking out from behind the crystal mountain. A tram was coming down from the mountain. It could contain refugees or tourists, he would greet either one with a warm welcome. Most of the citizens of the village were away now, plenty of room for a fresh cut of humanity to join him in this vision. A sustainable village should thrive on new citizens with new ideas.

Up on the hill he heard the first beats of the Full Moon Drum Circle. Slowly he made his way there, the glow of the fire drawing him ever closer. When he arrived at Sacred Earth Plaza the warmth enveloped him, not just from the flames, but the crowd as well. Dancers circled the fire, men and women touched by tribal rhythms. Two men were on the stage behind the circle, one twirling fire pots while another danced with a flaming baton. Randall took his customary seat on the edge of the stage, a raised platform with his back to the mountain overlooking the sea and the rooftops of the nearby houses. His tapered bass drum sat to his left and a talking drum called a Batá to his right. He picked one up and began to tap it gently, beating it louder as he fell into the rhythm of the community.

22

The conference room was empty, the time for meetings over. Anyone peeking in the entrance would see an empty conference room, that's all. Unless, of course, they had the gift of *Sight*. In that case, the astral form of Cameron Singh, visible to these few, would invite them to come in and have a seat beside him, perhaps share a moment of success.

"Why project myself in a thousand places when I can watch it all on these screens. It is a lot less effort to focus on a television screen than to create yet another astral body."

There were images from newsfeeds around the world. It was the opposite of what he first saw on these same screens. There were pictures of smiling people next to sustainable gardens. A young couple in obvious love was moving into their new crystal home. There was a report on power restoration, scenes of sustainable, renewable energy sources being built, including windmills, solar panels, waterwheels, and finally a giant power plant. Groups of volunteers assembled batteries and storage devices, embracing the opportunity to learn new skills that bolstered their pride and sense of self sufficiency.

There was a report of a new refinery that collected debris and garbage and returned electricity, producing more than it consumed, more than enough to power the recovery efforts. On the same site they manufactured and dispensed rechargeable batteries made from scrap, hoping to never again see them in a landfill or a hazardous material waste drop.

A community gathered around a banquet table enjoying a meal, a gardener telling everyone how he was able to grow so much so quickly. An algae farmer explained how easy it was to care for microscopic plants. When he was finished, his wife took over, sharing some of her best recipes, including how to make high energy power bars. There was story about an amusement park, a zoo for marine life where killer whales once performed for the amusement of crowds. Now it was a school, the arenas converted to classrooms where dolphin professors taught humans about a different way of life.

Congregations prayed in mosques, synagogues, chapels and churches throughout the land. People were worshiping in record numbers.

Cameron was not surprised to see his friends featured in a lot of the news. A band played in an open air park, Mel blowing notes through a crystal tuba. Kenji Alamoto and Nan Chi Han cut the ribbon in front of a new hybrid torus power plant. General Whiteweather was being sworn in as President of the United States, Juliana beside him as his First Lady. Stine showed an eager band of scientists a high speed animation example of Deep Time Ecology where a water well is built and a city grows up around it. Eventually, in his animation, it became crystal homes and farmland surrounded by a green landscape with food crops and trees in all directions. Animals returned to the land in thriving populations.

There were news media flashes, headlines that delivered the latest internet clickbait: "Population goes down to one billion, new birth control practices create a sustainable population." "World peace. Spiritual values thriving." "President Whiteweather signs new education bill: Free college and technical training for all." "Africa: The new superpower."

Singh took it all in, closing his eyes to the media, traveling deep within himself to a place beyond his most profound meditations. In his heart he saw Gaia. She spun in space, turning from dull gray and brown into a shining world of blue and green again. Dark shapes of negative energy were leaving the planet, their retreat channeled through a gauntlet of Galactic spaceships as they moved into a portal that led back to their own dark dimension. More than half of the city lights grew dim or went off completely, the Earth falling into a gentle stillness at night. The moon smiled down on her.

In Singh's heart she began to glow from within, an aura of health that told him Gaia had begun to fulfill her destiny and ascend to a higher dimension.

23

Chase sat in the easy chair behind the desk in his study. It was daylight outside but he had the curtains drawn, the door locked lest someone see the precious Triflux generator in front of him. Studying it carefully, he picked it up and turned it upside down. There was a switch. He flipped it and gently set it down. A smile came over his face, a sense of peace. He turned it over again, flipped the switch off and was back to scowling Chase. He flipped it again and smiled, off again and scowled. He finally set it down and pushed it aside.

"I don't see how this thing works," he said. "Guess I should have asked for a set of instructions."

THE END

Also by Nick Delmedico, available on line. Visit halfabook.com for more information.

Aliens vs Dinosaurs at the Beginning of Time. (co-authored with his son, Nick Delmedico) The World of the Dinosaur – 65 million years ago when giant beasts fought each other for dominance of the herd. One monarch has a vision of a better world in which dinosaurs cooperate and live in peace. But that peace is shattered when hostile aliens from another planet challenge the dinosaurs for dominion of the Earth. They collect the small ones, the children, taking them away to a distant laboratory where they can experiment on  them and find new ways to destroy the dinosaurs once and for all. King Rex finds his daughter is among the missing. As his world crumbles around him, as his enemies circle around him looking for weakness, he struggles to find a way to harness the power of flying without wings, His goal: to send an envoy of peace to he aliens to negotiate the release of the children. Failing that, to take the children back using an army of dinosaurs that have united behind him with one thought in mind: RESCUE THE CHILDREN.

Becky Jane: Memoir of an Incredible Life. In 2014, Becky was diagnosed with end stage esophageal cancer. Nick saw her through chemotherapy and radiation treatments. When the cancer returned in 2017, metastasized in her lower gut, she refused treatment choosing quality of life over quantity. He and his son left their jobs to take her on a final bucket tour. This is their story, a family driving towards an

inevitable destination that cannot be avoided. But if you live bravely, there can be many pleasant stops along the way. A 2017 Human Relations Indie Book Award Winner well worth reading.

Sword of Fire. Do angels die? A father tries to answer his daughter's questions even while he struggles with his own mortality. As an angel, he shouldn't worry about these things and neither should she. Except, as a survivor of the war between the angels, he knows the truth. With war inevitable in heaven, he is torn between siding with his brother Lucifer or with God, his Father and Creator. In the heat of battle, he rushes to God's side to catch the blood pouring from  a wound made by Satan's spear. This action creates the Holy Grail and draws him into the plight of the neutral angels as they attempt to smuggle the sacred relic out of heaven and hide it in a place of safety somewhere between heaven and hell.

Digital books available online:
Corporate Mercenaries
Could You Please Hold My Baby
Once Again, Prometheus

Thanks for reading!

www.ingramcontent.com/pod-product-compliance
Lightning Source LLC
Chambersburg PA
CBHW071343170626
46811CB00003B/967